Until
VIENNA

OTHER BOOKS AND AUDIOBOOKS
BY HEATHER B. MOORE
Women of the Book of Mormon: Insights & Inspirations
Christ's Gifts to Women
*Divinity of Women: Inspiration and Insights from Women
of the Scriptures*
Athena
Ruby's Secret
Tying the Knot

OTHER BOOKS AND AUDIOBOOKS
BY H.B. MOORE
Out of Jerusalem: Of Goodly Parents
Out of Jerusalem: A Light in the Wilderness
Out of Jerusalem: Towards the Promised Land
Out of Jerusalem: Land of Inheritance
Abinadi
Alma
Alma the Younger
Ammon
Daughters of Jared
Esther the Queen
The Moses Chronicles: Bondage
The Moses Chronicles: Deliverance
The Moses Chronicles: Exodus
Ruth
Anna the Prophetess
Deborah: Prophetess of God
Mary and Martha

OTHER BOOKS AND AUDIOBOOKS IN THE
ROMANCE ON THE ORIENT EXPRESS SERIES
It Started in Budapest by Julie Daines
Wrong Train to Paris by Jennifer Moore
Until Vienna by Heather B. Moore
Song of Salzburg by Jen Geigle Johnson (coming August 2021)

Until VIENNA

Romance on the Orient Express

HEATHER B. MOORE

Covenant Communications, Inc.

Cover photograph by Melea Nelson.
Visit www.meleanelson.com
Cover design by Michelle Fryer

Special thanks to Mark Nelson and the Heber Valley Railroad who provided the trains for the cover photoshoot.
For more information, visit www.hebervalleyrr.org

Published by Covenant Communications, Inc.
American Fork, Utah

Printed in the United States of America
First Printing: April 2021

28 27 26 25 24 23 22 21   10 9 8 7 6 5 4 3 2 1

ISBN 978-1-52441-542-6

PRAISE FOR
HEATHER B. MOORE

"In *Until Vienna*, Gigi and Clyde, both suffering from broken hearts, meet on an art tour. They become friends, and pledge to remain only that, even though a group of well meaning matchmakers thrusts the pair together at every turn. An entertaining cast of characters and an array of romantic settings make this a story not to be missed."

—Jennifer Moore, author *Wrong Train to Paris*

"A lovely story of second chances. Gigi and Professor Haskins have both been stung by past loves, but as they ride the Orient Express across Europe, the wonderful journey provides the perfect setting for their friendship to grow into something more. *Until Vienna* is a luxurious adventure full of heart and humor and loves of the greatest kinds."

—Julie Daines, author *It Started in Budapest*

"Get ready to laugh at all the humor in this beautiful romance. I'm in love with the quirky Aunt Rowena and her matchmaking failures that just might work!"
—Jen Geigle Johnson, author *Song of Salzburg* (coming August 2021)

FOR JULIE, JENNY, AND JEN
I'm blessed to call you friends.

ACKNOWLEDGMENTS

WHEN I WENT TO A publisher's meeting in 2019, I had little idea that a series idea would be born, then take off on wings of its own accord soon after. Julie Daines, Jennifer Moore, and Jen Geigle Johnson were all in attendance, and history was made in mere moments when we decided it would be fun to write a series together. Working on a long-term project with someone really exposes the core of that person. I am blessed that all of these women were wonderful to work with and their creativity was both inspiring and impressive. Julie Daines finished her book first, and since I hadn't even begun mine, I was a bit apprehensive to read it. I'd been part of the planning stages for the series as a whole, but what had Julie created from all of it? I needn't have worried because Julie's story was captivating, fun, and delightful to read. Of course that put the pressure back onto me to also rise to the occasion. Months later, when I had completed my own book, and read Jennifer's and Jen's, I felt absolutely blessed. And pleased. And excited to present the series to our readers.

Thank you to these good authors, who work hard at their craft and take pride and special care in their story creations.

Thank you to our publisher, who supported our ideas from the very beginning and encouraged us along the way.

Thank you to our editors, namely Ashley Gebert, who worked on my particular story and caught all the things and pushed my book to be stronger and more cohesive. Also, thanks to Kami Hancock, who had her hand in the entire project, keeping us all in line. Many thanks to Amy Parker, who is our champion in marketing. And our cover design team, including art director Margaret Weber, was stellar, as always. Many more at Covenant had a hand in the production of these books, and I'm so appreciative of that bridge from my hands to yours.

Thank you to my family for patiently listening to my "book talk" even when they can't keep track of whether I'm reading a book, researching a book, or actually writing one.

And thank you to the historians, artists, and archivists who have preserved history so we can once again visit it.

CHAPTER ONE

Summer 1900

EVER SINCE GIGI WAS OLD enough to know her name, she'd realized life wasn't fair. And she realized that her aunt, Rowena Georgina Ballard, always got her wish. But didn't Gigi's sixty-five-year-old aunt deserve to have her way when she'd seen a thing or two in life, had her own money to spend, and was in fair health?

Except when the wish interfered with Gigi's life. Rowena Georgina Ballard II's life, that was.

Yes, typically, sons were named after their fathers, and daughters might have a middle name after a mother or aunt or grandmother. But an entire name? Warranting a number after it?

Such was the fate of Gigi.

The second.

"Gigi!" her mother hollered from the bottom of the stairs of their London townhome. "Aunt Rowena will be here within the hour, and you've still to practice the sonata she wants to hear you play tonight."

"I'm on my way, Mother," Gigi called.

Gigi hid her sigh because her dear mother had the ears of a basset hound. If there was one thing the Ballard family did not do, it was disrespect the woman who held the purse strings for all of them. Since Father's death two years before, they'd been forced to sell their home, pay off debts, and move into this London town house owned by Aunt Rowena.

"You'd better go," Gigi's sister, Lillian, drawled from across the corridor, where her bedroom door was partly open.

Lillian Rose Ballard had a name not handed down from anyone in the family—a name to call her own.

She was also engaged to be married in three months' time to the esteemed Bart Anderson, who worked at a prestigious bank. This meant that Gigi was officially the least accomplished out of the entire Ballard clan. The age of twenty-four was almost unheard of to be single. A few decades ago, she would have been dubbed a spinster. In the year 1900, she had a little more leeway. But not much.

Lillian's recent engagement hadn't helped curb their mother's apprehension over her oldest daughter's fate.

But Gigi was completely content in her role as a part-time dressmaker. Her mother wouldn't let her work more than a few hours a day since she believed Gigi needed to be well rested for any social events. That included perfecting her piano playing so that her mother could demand a performance anytime they were in mixed company.

With another sigh, Gigi rose from her writing desk, where she'd been stitching piping on a sleeve. She wanted to present her design idea to Mrs. Stanton, the woman who ran the dress shop. Adding unique touches to clothing was something Gigi enjoyed doing; she just had to convince Mrs. Stanton of the value.

Walking into the corridor, she was surprised to see how advanced the day had become. The afternoon sun bathed the front entryway in gold and orange. No wonder her mother was on edge. She hurried down the stairs, then entered the drawing room where the piano sat. Once she settled onto the bench, smoothed out her full skirt, and adjusted her shirtwaist, she placed her hands on the ivory keys.

The notes of the sonata were light, and after a few times through, Gigi felt comfortable enough with it to please her mother. Aunt Rowena was a tad harder to please, and Gigi would not be spared any criticism from that corner.

Gigi was still practicing when the front knocker sounded. She paused as she listened for the butler's shuffling steps. Mr. Carson should have long since retired, but Aunt Rowena was paying his salary, so no one in the town house had a say in his employment.

The knocking sounded a second time before Carson reached the door and opened it.

The familiar murmured voices told Gigi that her aunt had arrived.

After only a handful of moments, Aunt Rowena swept into the drawing room wearing a wide hat topped with artificial flowers and feathers. The plum color of her dress matched the plum-dyed feathers on her hat, and her silver-threaded hair was done up in an elaborate pompadour. Her walking stick completed her bold outfit.

"There you are, Georgina," Aunt Rowena said. "You will not believe what I've come across. We must speak to your mother at once."

Gigi had no chance to reply because her mother appeared at that very moment.

"Rowena, how lovely that you're early."

"Ah, pish." Aunt Rowena waved a gloved hand before she took a seat on a wing-backed chair that had seen better days. "Hester, I've news to share." She opened her handbag and pulled out a brochure.

Gigi leaned forward as Aunt Rowena used some ceremony to open the brochure. She cleared her throat and began to read:

> *"Join Professor Clyde Haskins on the Orient Express for a tour of a lifetime. We will begin at the Exposition Universelle in Paris and spend a delightful day visiting the international art exhibition as special guests of Colonel Weston, the Commissaire Expert des Beaux-Arts. At each major stop along the journey, we will visit world-renowned museums, from the Louvre Museum in Paris all the way to the Hagia Sophia Museum in Constantinople. We will depart from the most important cities after spending a day or two in each splendid location. On the return trip, we will remain on the Orient Express. Once we arrive in Paris, we'll spend another three days exploring the Exposition."*

Gigi's mother looked duly impressed. Gigi, on the other hand, couldn't help but think of all the time and money this type of tour would take. Only the very wealthy could afford it. Someone like Aunt Rowena, to be sure, and those people who drove around in those shiny automobiles. What were they called? The carriage of the future?

"How fascinating," her mother murmured when Aunt Rowena had finished reading the brochure in its entirety, including the amenities on the Orient Express, such as world-renowned chefs and private berths in first class.

Aunt Rowena folded the brochure and, with a triumphant smile, said, "The members of my whist club are all going, save for Agnes, so we need a fourth player. And I have already booked passage. We leave next week."

"We?" her mother echoed.

"I'll need a companion, Hester," Aunt Rowena said. "Although I will be with my two friends, we are all older women. So we will need a younger person with us to fetch and carry our belongings if needed. Bring Lillian in, and we can begin to make plans."

"Lillian?" Mother asked. "She's planning a wedding, and this tour is an entire month long. There is no way that she—"

"Georgina, then." Aunt Rowena's light-blue eyes landed on Gigi.

Gigi straightened in surprise. "Me?"

Aunt Rowena waved a hand. "Yes, you. I don't expect you to appreciate this as much as Lillian would since you're always bent over a piece of lace or sagging hem, but I can't very well travel without a companion. What if there are unscrupulous men on this tour who wish to take advantage of a wealthy widow?"

"Unscrupulous men on an art museum tour?"

Aunt Rowena's wrinkles congregated into a frown. "Are you a parrot? I'll have you know that I'm quite the catch."

Gigi wouldn't laugh, not now. No, that would take place in her bedroom later. But now that she thought about it, there were probably plenty of older gentlemen who wouldn't mind being married to a wealthy woman no matter her personality.

Besides, Gigi wasn't one to judge. She had youth on her side, and she'd had not one offer. Not even Jimmy Dorsal. Everyone had thought he was sweet on her—but then he'd gone ahead and proposed to Mary Wright. It was all very well. Gigi hadn't been truly in love. More hopeful, she told herself. That's why she'd been disappointed. If she'd been in love with Jimmy Dorsal, she would have been devastated.

Nearly a year had passed since then, and she could barely remember the wave of his dark hair, the amused gleam in his crystal-blue eyes, the quirk of his mouth when he listened to one of her shop stories, and how when they danced, she felt like the most beautiful woman in the room . . .

And more recently, she'd had three different men pay attention to her, sending flowers, asking her on walks or rides, but then something would happen. Something that Gigi didn't understand. Each one had gone completely silent. First there was Richard Turley, a talented musician. Then there was Phillip Brandon, a banker. Yes, he was ten years older, but they had seemed to be a good match. Until they weren't.

Finally, there was Reggie Mann, who worked with his father at their general store. Gigi had liked him well enough, and she was just beginning to think he might propose when he'd sent a note around, apologizing profusely.

> *Dear Miss Ballard,*
>
> *I have enjoyed our acquaintance as of late. I must offer my most sincere apologies because I will have to break our upcoming plans. In addition, I will not be calling upon you again.*
>
> *My sincere wishes for your happiness,*
>
> *Reggie Mann*

"You are a catch for any distinguished gentleman," her mother soothed, patting Aunt Rowena's arm. "And Gigi would love to go with you."

Gigi frowned. Was this not her decision? Apparently not, because her mother and aunt had now moved on to discussing what needed to be prepared, purchased, and packed. Two weeks. They were leaving in two weeks.

"What about my job?" Gigi blurted. "I can't leave Mrs. Stanton in a bind."

Both women on the other side of the room stopped talking and looked at her as if she'd just declared that she'd turned into a horse.

Aunt Rowena's mouth twitched. "You cannot be serious, Georgina. This is the trip of a lifetime. Mrs. Stanton can survive among her fripperies and feathers without your help, I daresay. Isn't that right, Hester?"

Gigi's mother's face flushed, but she rushed to assure Aunt Rowena that she was indeed right.

Gigi's heart sank. Aunt Rowena always got her way. Twenty minutes ago, Gigi's life had been predictable and plain, just how she liked it. Now she'd be living in close quarters with her aunt and her aunt's whist club on a train. Well, them and unscrupulous older men.

CHAPTER TWO

THE BLUR OF THE PAST two weeks had finally caught up to Gigi as she stood before her half-packed trunk. Lillian and her mother were fussing over how many hats she should take. Unfortunately, hat boxes were large and took up a lot of room.

Her mother and Lillian resembled each other so much that oftentimes shopkeepers mixed them up. Their willowy figures, ebony hair, and brown eyes had contrasted with Gigi's father's stocky build, brown hair, and blue eyes—he was the parent Gigi had taken after. Instead of sporting striking looks like her sister and mother, Gigi had average brown hair that was quite dull in color and blue eyes that seemed to be the color of so many others. Oh, and the stocky build? Gigi was tall and . . . not exactly stocky, but definitely not willowy either.

This hat box debate had gone on far too long. So long, in fact, that Gigi was actually beginning to look forward to a month sequestered in a small sleeping compartment with her aunt.

"Two," Gigi said. "I'll take two hat boxes. I'll wear one hat to the train, and then I'll rotate three hats among the two boxes."

Her mother paused. "That might work."

"Three hats is not enough," Lillian stated as if she were the expert on packing for a train ride. "Aunt Rowena will have at least a dozen."

"But I'm not Aunt Rowena."

Lillian smiled. "No, you're not."

Gigi wasn't sure if the smile was a loving sister smile or a smile of irony. Needless to say, as soon as her sister and mother had vacated their helpful packing efforts, Gigi would be adding some of her own items. Her sketchbooks. Her piping, lace bits, and box of buttons. She couldn't take much extra fabric, but she'd add what she could in the cracks and crevasses between the other essential items being packed.

"What have you done, Gigi?" her mother practically screeched.

Gigi's stomach hollowed before she tracked her mother's raised finger pointing at the open wardrobe. There hung a silk ball gown that Lillian had worn last year to a few functions. Her mother had insisted that Gigi pack it even though Gigi had insisted right back that trains did not hold balls.

"I'm not taking a ball gown." Oh, and the creation was *pink*. A color to stand out for sure, and one that looked beautiful on Lillian. On Gigi, the pink merely made her look like a pale mannequin with no color to her skin.

Hester set her hands on her hips. She meant business.

Gigi sighed. "I doubt any of the other women are bringing ball gowns, Mother," she ventured. But her voice had lost its strength.

"Aunt Rowena mentioned specifically for you to bring a formal dress."

Gigi knew. She'd read the list Aunt Rowena had sent over. It was extensive, and so far, Gigi had been able to cut about a third of the items. Why hadn't she shut the wardrobe door before her mother and sister had sailed into her room?

Maybe . . . just maybe she could claim it ripped or stained if the occasion did arise to wear the fearsome thing. Then again, Gigi was a seamstress, so that excuse wouldn't quite work.

And . . . this was the third day of packing. The third day of debating. The third day of her headache. But once Gigi repacked the ball gown, her mother declared a headache of her own and blessedly retreated to her bedroom.

"Well? Don't you have somewhere to be?" Gigi said, looking over at her sister, who was busy rummaging through the face creams and perfumes and other makeup items Gigi was leaving behind.

Lillian looked up, her brown eyes the picture of absolute innocence. "Not particularly. I mean, there is the dinner tonight with Bart's family, but that's ages away."

"Just because I'm going to be gone for a few weeks doesn't mean you can use my toiletries. I'm still going to need them when I come back."

"Oh, I know," Lillian said, flashing a smile. "I'm only looking. Besides, I'm out of rose water, and you have plenty."

Gigi glared at her sister, but Lillian ignored her.

Lillian dabbed some of the rose water onto her neck, then her wrists. Satisfied, she straightened. "You're not going to wear that ball gown, are you?"

Gigi didn't answer. She became suddenly interested in rearranging the shoes on the edges of the trunk.

"You can hide it in my room if you want," Lillian offered. "I won't say a thing. Of course Aunt Rowena will blow her top, but you can deal with that later. Away from Mother."

"What?" Gigi said. "My perfect, beautiful sister is a rebel at heart?"

Lillian's dimple peeked out as she grinned. Oh, Lillian had dimples too, which only added to her already splendid features.

"I might be a little jealous of your trip," Lillian said. "Even if Bart had the money, he thinks art is boring and a waste. He doesn't understand how it can even be a profession."

This surprised Gigi. First, Lillian had never said anything negative about her fiancé, and second, Gigi hadn't known Bart was so averse to art.

"I'll write to you every day," Gigi offered. "You'll get minute details about the food and whist games and old-lady gossip."

Lillian laughed, but then she sobered. "Is it weak-minded to say that I'll miss you?"

Gigi blinked against the stinging in her eyes. In truth, as much as her sister and mother could get under her skin, they'd never been apart any length of time. "Not as pathetic as for me to say that I'll miss you."

Her sister laughed again, and then they were hugging.

"I just know you're going to come back having seen the world," Lillian said on a long sigh, "and you won't want to spend time with boring old me."

Gigi drew away from her sister. "Well, I might finally be interesting since you got all the beauty in the family."

Lillian normally took compliments to heart, but this time, she said, "*You're* beautiful, Gigi. You just don't know it yet."

Gigi went quiet at that and turned away.

Lillian touched her sleeve. "Gigi, maybe this trip will help you forget Jimmy Dorsal."

Gigi drew in her breath. Her sister knew not to speak of the man. Besides, nothing would ever make her forget. The humiliation had burrowed too deep for that. "I've already forgotten him." Gigi forced a smile on her face before she turned toward her sister again. "Jimmy who?"

Lillian laughed, but it wasn't quite genuine.

After the sisters' heart-to-heart, the packing went by swiftly, and the morning of departure arrived equally swiftly. It turned out that stepping onto the train that would take them to Paris and the beginning of the Orient Express adventure was much more bittersweet than Gigi had expected. She felt like she was letting down Mrs. Stanton, and now the wedding preparations that had seemed so tedious before held more appeal. Gigi would miss an entire month's worth.

At least Lillian had agreed to let Gigi make the wedding dress. She would sketch some sample designs on the train, and hopefully by the time she returned to London, she'd have a beautiful, original dress designed.

They met Aunt Rowena's two friends and whist partners at the London train station. The two women were of indeterminable age, although Gigi guessed they were in their early sixties. First, there was Irene Martin with her owlish eyes and silver hair. She was so thin that a stiff breeze might topple her should one arise.

Blanche Kenneth was the most friendly out of the two. She greeted Gigi with a hug and a kiss on her cheek. "You smell wonderful, Georgina. Is it rose water?"

"Yes," she began to say, but Blanche had already turned away to check her reflection in the windows of the train. Her immaculate hair was still in place. As they waited for boarding to start, Blanche kept up a running, and rather one-sided, commentary on the cleanliness of the station and her worries about the cleanliness of the train.

"Don't fuss over it, Blanche," Aunt Rowena said. "If there is a problem, then we will complain to the conductor."

The ferry ride and train ride from London to Paris were uneventful, unless one counted the number of times Aunt Rowena requested that her tea be taken back. *Three.* Gigi sensed a collective sigh of relief from the staff and the whist club as Aunt Rowena finally nodded her approval of the current cup of tea.

"Now," Aunt Rowena said. "I've brought a list."

Gigi wasn't surprised. Aunt Rowena thrived on lists, and Gigi was quite certain when the woman finally stepped from this life into the next, she'd have a to-do list for the Almighty.

Withdrawing a notebook from her traveling satchel, Aunt Rowena tapped her cane for . . . effect? Gigi had no idea.

"Our tour begins in Paris tomorrow," Aunt Rowena said, looking at each member of their party in turn. "We will meet Professor Haskins and the rest of the party at 11:00 a.m. for a light luncheon, then a private tour of the Louvre. Following that, we'll visit the Grande Palais art exhibit at the Paris Exposition."

"Should we eat before the light luncheon in case what we are served is inadequate?" Blanche worried.

"What?" Irene broke in. "Will there not be enough food?"

"I am sure there will be enough food," Gigi said. "The brochure promised luxury meals and unforgettable desserts."

Everyone looked at her.

"She's right," Aunt Rowena proclaimed. "We will be taken care of."

But Blanche's shoulders were still stiff, and Irene's brows had furrowed.

Gigi began to wonder, not for the first time, what she'd gotten herself into.

CHAPTER THREE

Dear Lillian,

> *I'm writing this in the early hours of the morning while in our Paris hotel. Aunt Rowena is fast asleep, and I wish I could go out and explore the shops and bakeries. Divine scents have made their way to our third-floor room. My stomach is protesting greatly. No matter. Today we will join the tour, and I'll finally meet Professor Haskins, the man Aunt Rowena has not stopped talking about . . .*

ELEVEN O'CLOCK CAME AND WENT, and still, Gigi and her group of women had not left the hotel. As Gigi paced the lobby, she had a sinking feeling about all of this. What if they missed the luncheon and the first museum tour? What would the professor and the others on the tour think of their gaggle of tardy women?

Meanwhile, Gigi was left to pace the lobby and observe the comings and goings of the hotel guests. Her eye was caught by current French fashions that some of the wealthier women wore. Gigi found an available seat and began to sketch one of the dresses from memory. She couldn't very well sketch when the lady would notice her. Soon she became so caught up in her sketching that she didn't see Aunt Rowena and her whist friends arrive.

"Are you ready?" Aunt Rowena said. "We've got to make haste."

Gigi popped up from her seat and put her notebook into her handbag. The women hurried out of the hotel, as fast as women in their sixties wearing heeled boots could hurry. The walk was short because they were meeting in the next hotel over. As they entered the next hotel, which was full of Turkish rugs and sparkling chandeliers, Aunt Rowena immediately inquired after the luncheon group.

Gigi wondered about her role in this group of ladies. They seemed to be on their own schedule and perfectly capable of locating the first part of the tour. Aunt Rowena even spoke French to the concierge. Gigi had hoped she'd be more useful to the ladies than just a fourth whist player. But as it was, she was following after them like the runt of a puppy litter.

"This way." The concierge had an impeccable mustache and a deep-red uniform. "The second course is being served, but we can bring out both courses at once for your group."

"Wonderful!" Blanche exclaimed.

"I'm ever so hungry, but I'm not sure I can eat any escargots," Irene muttered.

Gigi followed the group to a set of double doors, which the concierge opened with a flourish before leading them inside.

Gigi's first impression was that the tour group was full of women all around her aunt's age, although there appeared to be three men—two older men, likely with their wives, and a man who must be in his thirties. This younger man rose to his feet immediately and strode toward them.

His hair was nearly white, not because he was an elderly gentleman, but because it was a blond color lighter than a birch tree. He wore a dark jacket and gray trousers paired with highly polished black shoes. An energy exuded from him, and Gigi wondered if these older folks would be able to keep up with him.

"Welcome," he said, coming to a stop in front of their little group. His hair might have been the lightest Gigi had seen on a person, but his eyes were a dark hazel. "I'm Clyde Haskins. We're pleased you could join us. You must be Mrs. Rowena Ballard."

Aunt Rowena beamed. "Yes." She nodded at the others. "These are my friends that I wrote you about. Irene Martin and Blanche Kenneth. My niece also agreed to come—Georgina Ballard."

Gigi moved out from behind the group, and Professor Haskins's gaze shifted to her. His brows shot up, and Gigi didn't know what to make of it. Why was he surprised? Because she would be the youngest in the group?

"Lovely to meet you," Blanche said, and the professor's attention was diverted to the main group again.

"Welcome all," he said. "Now, let me show you your table, and soon, toward the end of the meal, I'll explain the itinerary for the rest of the day."

Gigi stayed close to Aunt Rowena because, again, Professor Haskins cast her a curious look. Was it really so odd that a younger person would join his tour, especially since she was accompanying her aunt?

She tried not to look at him because his frequent glances were starting to bother her. She kept her attention on her meal of a delicious onion soup and a beef dish that Aunt Rowena informed everyone was called *boeuf bourguignon*. Everything was quite delicious. Of course, they were in Paris, so perhaps that was a given.

Gigi listened absently to Aunt Rowena's friends discussing each dish, and Blanche worried about "foreign food" not sitting right with her stomach. Gigi stole a few glances at the other tables of people. By their dress and manners, they all seemed to be English. No foreigners among them.

As the dessert was brought out, a beautiful chocolate soufflé, Professor Haskins took his place at the front of the room. "Welcome again, everyone. It's wonderful to meet each of you, and I'm looking forward to our shared experiences." His smile was warming, and Gigi imagined that he'd have no trouble keeping his audience captive. All of the women at her table had forgotten their desserts and were now focused on him.

"A few years ago, I was taking the Orient Express as a sort of vacation between semesters at the university, and I fell into a conversation with an older married couple on the train." He gave another warm smile, and all of the women at Gigi's table smiled back. "They were enjoying their train ride, but they were also interested in stopping at the main stations and exploring each city. Because of their age, they didn't feel comfortable navigating all the modern changes to the cities and wished for a younger, more experienced guide. That discussion led to the idea of providing that service to others. So for two months out of the summer each year, I lead two different groups. You are the second this year."

Aunt Rowena clasped her hands together, hanging on his every word.

The professor paused. "Because of this couple, who said they were in their twilight years and wanted a guided tour, I began the Twilight Tour. It allows for the members of the tour to interact with others their age and enjoy each other's company."

Ah, Gigi thought. Twilight. For older people. And here she was.

A few of the people at the other tables glanced at her, but Gigi forced a nonchalant smile and tried not to be bothered. She hadn't come on this trip to be social with people her own age anyway. Whenever she wasn't with her aunt, she'd be working on her designs.

"Art has impacted all of our lives, but often we only hear about art or read about it," the professor continued. "This tour will give you a chance to view famous art in person. An experience that is incomparable."

The professor talked more about the displays they'd visit at the Louvre, and Gigi tried to pay attention. She really did. But all sorts of emotions were crashing through her. Yes, her aunt had invited her, but once again, she was in a situation where she didn't truly fit.

And it would last for a month.

Professor Haskins concluded his speech, and everyone finished their desserts. The professor had hired two carriages to take the group to the museum, so after a flurry of activity, Gigi climbed into one of the carriages with her group and a few others. Professor Haskins took the rear carriage with the rest of the members.

Some of the streets were snarled with traffic—wagons, carriages, carts, and even a few automobiles—but Gigi didn't mind. She gaped at the scenery, the buildings, and especially the people.

"Oh, goodness, there are so many . . . foreigners," Blanche half whispered.

"It's the exposition, mind you," Irene said with authority.

As they neared the Louvre, Gigi grasped her hat and tilted her head up to see the top turrets of the massive building.

"It's more beautiful than I remember," Aunt Rowena said, awe in her voice. "I am so glad I get to see it once more before I die."

Gigi snapped her head around to look at her aunt. "Why would you say such a thing?"

Aunt Rowena patted Gigi's hand. "I'm no spring chicken any longer, Georgina."

The words did nothing to ease her mind. She'd never heard her aunt speak of her demise. It was disconcerting to say the least. The carriages slowed, and Gigi disembarked, then made sure her aunt and her friends got down from the carriage all right.

After helping Aunt Rowena, who seemed strangely out of breath, Gigi turned to help Irene.

"Thank you for your help," a man said behind her.

She knew it was Professor Haskins; she already recognized his voice.

She turned and lifted her chin to meet his gaze. "It's no trouble."

"Thank you all the same, Miss Ballard. Or shall I call you . . ." His eyes weren't exactly green or brown but a mix with flecks of gold. The edge of his mouth had lifted, but he still had that puzzled look in his eyes.

Was it really so off the mark to accompany her aunt, one who needed a cane, by the way? "Miss Ballard is fine."

"She's named after me," Aunt Rowena announced for anyone who cared to hear. "Rowena Georgina Ballard. I go by Rowena, and she goes by Georgina."

"Yes," Gigi murmured. "Or Gigi is fine too." She didn't know why she'd added that bit. It wasn't like she'd be friends with any members of the tour beyond this month's experience.

"Do we have to stand in that line?" Blanche asked, drawing everyone's attention to the congregation of people.

"We already have our entrance booked and our tour time scheduled," Professor Haskins said. "Follow me."

The group followed the professor to a door where a guard let them inside after verifying the professor's credentials. The moment Gigi stepped into the hallways of the Louvre, she was transfixed. They walked from room to room. The art, sculptures, and pieces of exquisite work sent awe drumming through her.

Throughout the next two hours, she felt the professor's puzzled gaze on her more than once. This was getting ridiculous, she decided. So when the first opportunity presented itself, she was determined to speak to him. She had to wait until they were in line to see a display and the professor stepped back so the group could move forward and get a closer look.

Gigi joined the professor where he stood apart from the rest. Keeping her gaze on the Egyptian statues, she whispered, "I'm here with my aunt, in case you're wondering why I've come at all."

Professor Haskins's gaze slid to hers, then refocused on the sculpture everyone was viewing. "Anyone is welcome on the tour, Miss Ballard."

"I am sure that is true in theory, but you made it clear it was for those in their twilight years." She felt his hesitation, as if he were choosing his words carefully.

"You think I'm bothered that a younger person is part of this tour?"

He was direct, and so she would be as well. "Are you not?"

This time, Professor Haskins turned fully toward her. They were standing rather close after all, and she hadn't realized how close until his complete gaze was upon her. "I am not bothered in the least."

"Professor Haskins," she continued in a low tone, "you've frowned at me more than my mother did when I was a child getting into scrapes."

The professor's mouth curved. "Scrapes? Such as?"

"You are changing the subject, sir."

His smile still grew, but it seemed he'd understood the earnestness of her question. His gaze flitted across her face as if he were studying it. "When I saw you at the luncheon, I had a sudden flash of familiarity. As if we've met before. But that is quite impossible, don't you agree? I haven't been to social events for years."

"Well . . . you don't look familiar to me." Perhaps it was a reticent comment, but it was the truth. "Your, uh, person is hard to miss. So I am sure I would have known had we met before."

His brows shot up at this, but there was amusement in his eyes. "Explain yourself, Miss Ballard."

The heat in her neck could only mean one thing: she was about to blush. She looked toward the sculpture again, thanking the stars above that these specific sculptures were not nudes.

When she looked at him, she found his gaze still upon her. "I have never seen hair your color." She didn't know what his reaction would be, but it wasn't what happened.

Professor Haskins laughed. Out loud.

Three women in front of them immediately turned and hushed the man.

This made Gigi laugh, although she was much more in control than the professor. And she quickly schooled her expression and tamped back her laughter. Too late, though. Aunt Rowena had noticed, and now her cane was tapping on the floor as she made her way toward Gigi.

"Excuse me," Professor Haskins murmured, his voice full of mirth.

Gigi didn't dare track where he was going, although she assumed it was someplace to compose himself. That thought only made her want to laugh again, but the feeling quickly died at the stern expression on her aunt's face.

"Georgina," Aunt Rowena hissed as soon as she reached her side. "You're causing a disturbance."

"Sorry, Aunt," Gigi said. "I didn't mean to make him laugh."

Aunt Rowena narrowed her pale-blue eyes. "Were you *flirting*, Georgina?"

Gigi held back a gasp. "Of course not."

Then her aunt leaned close and whispered next to her ear, "I wouldn't mind if you did, my dear, because I have it on good authority that he is a man of high quality. And I promised your mother I'd keep you free from any nefarious gentlemen."

Now Gigi's chest was heating up. "I would never, uh, fraternize with nefarious men."

"Smart girl," Aunt Rowena said. "Now, don't make it so obvious that you are interested. Discretion is much more attractive."

The heat had certainly traveled to her cheeks by now. "I did not mean to flirt. He is probably married anyhow."

Aunt Rowena tapped her chin. "I will find out. Somehow."

Please don't, Gigi wanted to say.

"What are we doing?" Irene asked in a rather loud whisper, joining the two of them.

"Nothing," Gigi said at the same time her aunt said, "Matchmaking."

"Matchmaking?" Blanche said with glee. When had she joined the circle?

"We need to put together a list of questions for Professor Haskins," Aunt Rowena said in an authoritative voice that was not at all quiet.

Fortunately, the main group had moved on to the next display, and only other strangers were present now.

"No list," Gigi said. "Please. I am not looking for a match on this tour." She hoped her voice had been firm enough, but the glances the women exchanged gave Gigi little hope that her wishes would be abided by.

CHAPTER FOUR

GIGI MANAGED TO AVOID ANY personal interaction with Professor Haskins for the remainder of the Louvre visit. She didn't miss the knowing glances of the women who were all now surveying the professor.

Poor man.

Poor *her*.

This tour would not be enjoyable if Gigi was always avoiding the professor and trying to prevent her party's tongues from wagging.

Back into the carriages they went, and the professor instructed the drivers where to take them to best avoid the main crowds at the Paris Exposition. The energy humming from him reminded Gigi of a group of young boys who played at the park near her home. Always moving, always alert.

Once they arrived at the location where they could be led to the Grande Palais, Gigi's neck ached from craning it to see all the wonders. The Eiffel Tower had been painted yellow. Imagine that. And there was the Grande Roue, which had to be at least one hundred meters high.

"Now, everyone," the professor was saying to the gathered group.

Gigi tried to pay attention.

"We will each get an iced lemonade," he said. "It is wonderfully refreshing."

Gigi had to agree, and she felt reenergized by the time they stepped into the art exhibit. The professor had explained that living artists around the world had spent months, some even years, preparing a piece to be displayed. She walked slowly with Aunt Rowena, inspecting painting after painting.

She stayed extra long in front of a landscape done in an impressionist style. The country house in the painting had blue shutters and flowerpots on either side of the door. The artist's talent with light was impressive, and her gaze was drawn to the details of the stones that made up the house and the nearby wall. Beneath a tree were two figures—lovers? The surrounding landscape only added to the feeling of romance with the orchids and lavender fields, flanked by majestic mountains in the distance. The entire painting had a dreamy quality, and it was as if Gigi had been transported to another time, another place. Her gaze shifted to the artist's signature in the corner of the painting, but she did not recognize the name.

"The artist is from Provence," the professor said. "I have it on exclusive authority that this is the first showing of his work. So you might consider yourselves blessed to be witnesses to it on this day."

"Ah, lovely," Aunt Rowena said. "How much is the artist asking for it?"

"It is not for sale," a deeper, older voice said.

Everyone turned.

"This is Colonel James Weston," the professor announced in a proud voice. "Colonel, this is Mrs. Rowena Ballard and her niece, Miss Ballard."

The colonel gave each woman a firm handshake. "Welcome to the exhibit. I am happy to answer any of your questions. But the painting in question is—shall we say—not authorized to be discussed at length."

"I love a good mystery," Aunt Rowena said. "Can we at least meet the artist?"

"He is not here," the colonel said but offered nothing else. "Might I show you a fine portrait that I think you'll find interesting?"

And the rest of the hour proceeded with a personal escort from the colonel. Gigi was most impressed, and she was sorry when it was time to leave. She was much looking forward to a return visit to the exposition. But they still had to return to their hotel, freshen up for the next part of their journey, then meet at the *Gare de l'Est* station to catch the 6:25 p.m. train.

This time around, Gigi insisted that they all be an hour early, which meant they ended up being thirty minutes early. Thankfully the uniformed porters were in abundance and very efficient in transporting all of the luggage onto the train with the gold crests painted on the side of the train cars.

She was surprised at how many people were coming and going. But the noise and bustle didn't detract from the beauty of the elegant columns, the interior archways, and the majesty of the half-rosette window presiding over more than two dozen platforms.

They found their tour group quickly, which brought Gigi immense relief.

"Is everything in order?" the professor asked, approaching.

"We are here in one piece, and our luggage has been taken by the porters," Aunt Rowena said. "Oh, look at those uniforms. What a sight."

Gigi followed her aunt's gaze to see that, indeed, the conductors of the Orient Express wore fine navy suits with brass buttons. A conductor stood at each entrance to the Wagons-Lits train cars, waiting to assist.

The train whistle sounded, and the professor ushered everyone toward the train.

Stepping onto the train was like entering a world of luxury. The conductor of their train car was a mustachioed man about an inch shorter than Gigi. He first showed Blanche and Irene their berth, then next to it, he opened the door to Gigi and her aunt's berth.

In their train compartment, the gas lights cast a warm glow about the space. Rich velvet drapes prevented the lights of the station from coming into the berth. Two bunks were folded, forming couches. They'd be adjusted into beds later in the evening.

Aunt Rowena didn't unpack a thing but sank onto her couch. "I must rest for an hour, Georgina," she said. "Can you be sure I don't oversleep?"

"Of course," Gigi said. This meant she needed to find a way to stay awake no matter what. While her aunt rested, Gigi slipped out into the corridor and made her way to the lounge car, which was just before the dining car.

In the lounge car, there were a couple of couches, and tables were grouped with other chairs. One table was occupied with three people playing a game of cards. Another had a man sitting and reading a newspaper.

Gigi sat near a window and gazed out at the darkened landscape. The lights of the city were fading fast to be replaced by nearly dark rural neighborhoods.

"You are traveling alone, miss?"

The male voice was accented, and she looked up to see a tall man standing nearby. Was he French? His black jacket and black trousers matched the black of his hair and bushy mustache, and he held a curvy pipe in his hand as if he were about to smoke it.

"I am here with my aunt and her friends," Gigi said, although she wasn't sure she should be quite so open to a complete stranger. His clothing was elegant and bespoke of wealth, but he could be anyone.

"Ah." The gentleman took a drag on his pipe and exhaled the smoke.

Gigi frowned.

"Are you traveling all zeh way to Constantinople?"

Gigi stilled. Was he Russian? That accent . . . and why was he so interested? The claims from her aunt about needing to be on guard against nefarious older gentlemen came back to Gigi's mind. She'd thought her aunt was being paranoid and quirky, but now . . .

"Yes," Gigi said, because this man could probably find out such a detail in another way. But something propelled her to keep talking, something she couldn't explain. "My aunt wanted to do this tour—she loves all art, you see. Since she uses a cane and sometimes doubts her physical abilities, she invited me."

Another inhale followed by a puff of smoke.

"And do you love art, miss?"

"I enjoy art," Gigi said. "Although I haven't spent much time studying it."

"Vhat do you study?" His dark eyes peered at her as if he were truly interested.

"I'm a dressmaker," Gigi said.

"Ah, an art in and of itself."

"I suppose so," Gigi said, although she hadn't quite thought of it that way. She was still trying to figure out this man. He had not introduced himself, and he had not asked her name either.

Her attention was caught by another man entering the lounge car. This man she recognized. Professor Haskins had changed into a more formal jacket, and his eyes landed on her immediately.

The man with the pipe seemed to notice and took a step back.

Professor Haskins reached him in a few strides. "Nicholas."

"Professor."

The two men shook hands, then Nicholas nodded to Gigi. "Welcome to zeh Orient Express. I vill leave you to zeh evening." He quickly walked out of the lounge car.

Professor Haskins settled onto the couch opposite Gigi, as if it were a normal thing to do and they were close acquaintances. He took off his hat and set it upon the table between them. Once again, she was struck by his white-blond hair, a stark contrast to his dark brows and dark eyes.

"Do you know that man?" she asked, shifting her gaze from the hazel eyes of the professor to the golden landscape outside. The sun had fallen behind the horizon, and the golds would soon be replaced by twilight blue.

"I've met him on previous trips."

"Does he work on the train?" Gigi asked.

Professor Haskins didn't reply at first but signaled a waiter. "I'll have a coffee. And the lady will have . . . ?"

When both pairs of eyes turned upon her, she said, "Tea, please."

After the waiter left, Professor Haskins answered. "Nicholas doesn't work on the train. He is a frequent traveler from what I can see."

Gigi's questions still weren't answered.

"I'm sorry for laughing at the museum," the professor said. "Was your aunt really so dismayed?"

So, he was being direct again. "She was dismayed until . . ." No, Gigi should not go further with that sentence.

But Professor Haskins's gaze had turned curious, and he tilted his head. "Until what, Miss Ballard?"

The drinks were delivered, offering a small reprieve. When Professor Haskins told the waiter to add both drinks to his tab, Gigi couldn't allow it.

"No, please," she told the waiter. "I insist that mine be on my tab. Thank you."

The waiter bowed and left.

"I was happy to put it on my tab," the professor said in a low tone.

"Thank you for your offer," Gigi said. "But I don't want anyone in our tour to speculate."

His brows arched, and Gigi had to look away from the intensity of his hazel gaze.

The professor picked up his coffee. "Are you going to answer my question about your aunt?"

Gigi exhaled. "My aunt is creating a list about you."

His hand paused halfway to his mouth. "A list?"

"Really, I shouldn't even mention it because it will only put weight onto something that shouldn't have any weight at all."

"I am intrigued, Miss Ballard." He took a small sip of his coffee, then set it on the table between them.

Gigi didn't want to continue, but she'd gotten this far, and she might as well nip this issue in the bud on the first night of the tour. "You know how older women are—all their speculating about young people and who will marry whom."

Professor Haskins's gaze shifted away, and he seemed to be staring at something unseen.

"You can completely ignore any meddling," Gigi said. "I know I will. Women are quite used to this sort of thing, so I'm sorry if this puts you in a difficult position."

It took another moment for his gaze to return to hers. He studied her face in that disconcerting way of his, the one that made the heat return to her neck and threaten to travel to her cheeks.

"Rest assured, sir," she began in an undertone, "I have no designs on any man. Not you or any other. I have other things to focus on."

His mouth twitched. "Such as?"

"My profession as a dressmaker."

The professor nodded, as if he understood perfectly.

"Besides, someone has to take care of my mother as she advances in years. My sister will be married in a few months, and then it will all be left to me."

"And your father?"

"Deceased two years ago."

He dipped his head. "My condolences."

She nodded, then picked up her tea. The robust taste was exactly what she needed right now. She took a swallow, then set the teacup down. Why hadn't she brought a book or something? Or her notebook? All she could do was pretend the darkening landscape outside was fascinating.

"You are a very loyal daughter," the professor said. "Your mother is fortunate to have you."

Gigi didn't like that this was turning into a compliment about her person. "Without a father in the household, someone needs to keep her head. I've been made a fool once in romance, and once is enough for me. Whatever my aunt may or may not say to you, about *me*, please know it does not come from me."

"That was quite a declaration," Professor Haskins said with a smile.

Her stomach didn't know whether to tighten with renewed anxiety or relax with relief that he found this amusing. "I've been known to speak my mind."

His smile widened. "Indeed."

"Is this entertainment for you?"

"Quite." He tilted his head. "And you?"

His smile was making her want to smile back. "I suppose that's one way to look at it."

"So, you are a successful dressmaker, without attachment, and you are your aunt's companion on this tour." His thumb traced the outside of his coffee cup.

"That sums it up," Gigi said. "And you, Professor?"

"As you said, I am a professor." His mouth held a faint smirk. "Of course, success is to be determined. But I am without attachment, although I have been played the fool too." Professor Haskins leaned back on the couch. "So you see, Miss Ballard, I'm a confirmed bachelor and intend to stay that way. No offense to you or any other woman on my tour or anywhere else. Do you think your aunt will be crushed?"

Gigi laughed. "She'll be extremely crushed. And believe me, I'm not offended in the least. I just wish a woman could so easily declare herself a bachelor too and be respected for it. The word *bachelor* carries a distinguished tone to it, whereas the female counterpart is . . . derogative. Being a *spinster* doesn't sound as appealing as being a confirmed bachelor."

The professor's eyes seemed to be dancing with amusement. "Surely there is a term better than *spinster*?"

"Bachelorette?" they both said at once.

Now the professor laughed.

Gigi decided on the spot that she quite enjoyed making him laugh. And it was even better knowing that neither he nor she was looking for any sort of attachment. Although, she was curious as to his past—the one woman who'd made him a fool. As for herself, she wasn't too keen to speak of Jimmy Dorsal.

"I think we have a deal, Miss Ballard," Professor Haskins said, still grinning. He leaned forward and extended his hand to shake hers.

"I believe we do." Gigi grasped his hand in hers. "Which deal are we shaking on?"

"To remain in our bachelor-bachelorette corners despite what your aunt throws at us."

He was still shaking her hand slowly, and Gigi ignored the warmth of his skin against hers and how her arm had pebbled with goose pimples. "Excellent," she said. "We must be strong, we must be brave, and we must be noble."

Professor Haskins's brows quirked with merriment. "Is that our motto then?"

"Do you have a better one?" she teased.

"I do not," he said. "Yours is perfect. This deserves a toast."

He released her hand. She reached for her teacup, then raised it to meet his coffee cup.

Their glasses clinked, a signal to the start of the next twenty-nine days in which they'd both work to stave off her aunt's advances.

CHAPTER FIVE

Dear Lillian,

We've officially boarded the Orient Express. Oh, what a train. I've seen pictures and advertisements of course, but the reality is truly amazing. The dark paneled corridors are of the finest wood. The plush carpeting is like a cloud beneath my feet. And although the sleeping quarters are small, as expected on a train, they've not forgotten any luxury. Beautiful velvet drapes, gilded mirrors, and brocade couch coverings. A conductor assigned to our train car who awaits to assist us with any little thing. Oh, and I must tell you about Professor Haskins. He is younger than I expected. Thirty perhaps? And his hair . . . goodness. It's so blond that it's nearly white. Aunt Rowena is already making mention of matchmaking. Heaven help me. Send prayers . . .

It took three tries for Gigi to rouse her aunt. Gigi almost gave up, but then she realized her aunt would wake naturally at some point during the night and be hungry.

"Oh goodness," Aunt Rowena said when she was finally roused. "I feel like I've been trampled by one of those bay horses. Everything aches. Give me a few moments to get ready."

Gigi returned to the new sketch she'd started of a man's formal suit. It wasn't what she usually worked on, but she would also add a woman by his side. She hadn't decided on the shape the dress would take yet.

She looked up when Aunt Rowena drew in a sharp breath of air.

"Are you all right?"

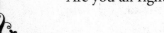

"Fine," Aunt Rowena said. "I must have slept wrong. Now, have you heard of the book *Dracula*? Irene was telling me that it's deliciously creepy."

Gigi shook her head. She might have been more concerned with her aunt's complaints, but with her cheerful chatter, Gigi decided it was nothing. Once Aunt Rowena had refreshed herself, they headed out of the berth and into the corridor. They bypassed the lounge car, and it took Gigi only a quick glance to determine that neither the mysterious Nicholas nor the professor was in sight.

A uniformed conductor stood at the entrance of the dining cart. He greeted them in French, then English. When Aunt Rowena responded in English, he said, "Very well, Madame Ballard, please follow me."

The dining car was pristine and elegant. The dining tables seated four people each. Crisp white tablecloths were topped with fine china and crystal wine glasses. Even the cloth napkins were elegantly folded.

When her aunt was finally ready, they joined Aunt Rowena's whist friends at a table. Blanche was decked out in enough diamonds to rival Queen Victoria, and Irene looked as if she'd taken a long nap on one side of her hair. The flatness of one side rivaled the poof of the other side.

They were immediately brought menus by a waiter and were asked for their drink orders. Gigi tried not to look around for Professor Haskins, but her gaze continually strayed to the entrance of the dining car as she anticipated his arrival. He was late, or maybe he wasn't coming.

Dinner was served like in any other fine dining restaurant, and her dinner companions oohed over the choices. Gigi ordered a chicken dish, and just as the waiter left to place their table's orders, Professor Haskins entered the dining car.

He was dressed as he had been during their conversation, but somehow he looked taller and more imposing. Gigi watched as he stopped at each table occupied by their tour group and exchanged pleasantries. She really shouldn't be staring, so she tried to tune back in to what her aunt was telling the other women about what time they needed to meet for breakfast in the morning.

"That's too early for me," Irene said. "When I travel, I need extra sleep."

"If I don't eat by eight in the morning, I'll earn myself a severe headache," Blanche countered.

And then he was there. At their table.

"Good evening, ladies," Professor Haskins said in his smooth tone.

The conversation halted, and everyone looked at him.

"What have you ordered for dinner?" he continued.

"I've decided to try the pork loin," her aunt said. Her words were soon followed by the other ladies declaring their menu choices.

Gigi hid a smile at the enthusiastic responses of each of the ladies.

"Georgina ordered the chicken," Aunt Rowena announced. "She always orders chicken, even though I've advised her to try something new."

Professor Haskins's gaze connected with hers, and she could see the amusement in his eyes.

An unspoken understanding passed between them, and Gigi barely contained a smile.

"I can't abide chicken," Blanche said. "I once saw a chicken slaughtered, and I lost my appetite." And that redirected the conversation once again.

Then the most curious thing happened: Professor Haskins winked at Gigi before turning his attention to Irene, who was talking about a study she'd read of how many nutrients were in chicken. Gigi felt her pulse spike, but she told herself it was nothing. She and the professor were in cahoots with each other. That was all.

When he excused himself after a moment to speak with others in the tour, the women were so caught up in comparing recipes for raspberry trifle that they hardly noticed the professor's absence.

As the meal progressed, Gigi wondered if fortune had smiled upon her and her aunt had forgotten about her list.

But her hope was soon dashed while they were waiting for dessert, and Aunt Rowena pulled out her notebook. "Now, ladies. Listen to this list and see if there is anything to add."

"What list is this?" Blanche asked.

"The one about the professor," Irene said, her brows rising above her owlish eyes.

Gigi's ears burned as the women at the table leaned in, their eyes locked on Aunt Rowena's notebook.

"Number one, is the professor attached? Married? Engaged? Widowed?"

"He wears no ring," Irene said.

"That doesn't mean a thing," Blanche countered.

Irene huffed. "Surely he would have spoken of his wife if he was married."

Gigi's head was spinning. "He's not married."

The three women all snapped their gazes to her.

"And how do you know this?" Aunt Rowena said in a voice that was too loud to be kept private.

Gigi winced. "We, ah, had a conversation in the lounge car while you were resting."

Blanche's eyes widened. "Alone?"

"No," Gigi was quick to say. "We were both in the lounge car at the same time, and others were present. It was nothing. Really." She waved a hand. "Proceed with your list."

Aunt Rowena was positively beaming, and she made great ceremony of returning to her list. "Number two, how financially prepared is the professor to support a wife and children?"

Gigi pressed her lips together. She was not going to burst out that of course a university professor could support a family. She also wouldn't add that she planned on continuing her own dressmaking career whether or not she married. That insight might add more fuel to these women's plans.

"Wait a minute," Blanche said, clasping her hands atop the table. "What do you mean by financially prepared?"

"Why, he should have plenty of investments," Aunt Rowena said.

"In gold," Irene added, patting her hair as if that would help its disarray.

Everyone looked at her. Aunt Rowena frowned. Opened her mouth. Closed it. Then turned back to her list. "Number three." She held up a finger. "And listen up; this is important. The professor must be in good standing with his community and place of employment."

"He's a wonderful man," Irene said, her voice a bit dreamy. "I've no doubt he's in good standing wherever he goes. You can tell by the way he walks. Very proper."

The conversation had started out in hushed tones, but now . . . surely others could hear them.

Something prickled at the back of Gigi's neck.

She turned her head slightly, and her breath caught. He was sitting at the next table over, and even though he appeared focused on the conversation at his table, Gigi had no doubt that he'd likely heard every word. She stifled a groan. What must he think of this table of meddling women?

Just before she turned her head back to look at her aunt, his gaze shifted. For a brief moment, their eyes connected. The edge of his mouth lifted. He *had* heard. Their gazes held a moment longer, and something passed between them—an understanding that this was only part of their original agreement to be good sports.

They'd both agreed to be strong, brave, and noble. Which step was this in the process?

She gave a nearly imperceptible nod to the man, then returned to the conversation. From her peripheral vision, she saw the smile playing on his lips, and she realized a smile was playing upon her lips as well.

"Number four . . ." Aunt Rowena looked at Gigi expectantly.

"Yes?" Gigi said, extremely aware that everything she said could be overheard by the professor himself.

"This is a delicate matter," Aunt Rowena said, "and possibly not for young ears."

Blanche tutted. "Should she cover her ears?"

"Or leave the table," Irene declared.

"I could sing a song in her ear while you speak so she can't hear."

Gigi blinked. "Perhaps it shouldn't be on the list, then. If there is something too sensitive for me to know about a man, then perhaps it is the wrong man."

"Oh, it's nothing like that," Aunt Rowena hastened to say. "It's . . . well . . ." She cupped a hand about her mouth, and in a very quiet voice, she said, "He must be virile."

None of the women at the table moved or spoke. In fact, the entire dining car seemed to go silent at that moment. Or perhaps it was because Gigi suddenly couldn't hear anything but a strange rushing sound in her ears as if she'd bent very, very close to a river.

"That is so important," Irene said in an equally quiet voice, her owl eyes growing, if possible, even wider.

"You will want children," Blanche added in an authoritative voice, touching the diamond necklace at her throat.

"And you will want enjoyment in—"

"Irene, hush!" Aunt Rowena hissed. "That is quite enough. We will now move on to number five."

Number five . . . Gigi was still trying to comprehend number four. How did her aunt plan on ascertaining all of these things about the professor, or any man, for that matter?

There was no way Gigi could turn to look at Professor Haskins now. Not if someone offered her ten thousand pounds. But she needn't have worried because from her peripheral vision, she saw the professor rise and hurry out of the dining car as if he were on an urgent errand. Was there an emergency?

Then, it dawned on her. He'd been so mortified by number four that he'd rushed to pack his belongings and would get off at the next stop, never to be seen again and never to lead another tour group.

"I must . . ." Gigi began. She couldn't even form the words. "Excuse me, I'll be back in a moment."

She had to find him, to stop him before he abandoned the group, to apologize at the very least, and to possibly disappear off the train herself. But as she hurried along the corridor into the next train car, she worried that he'd already returned to his berth, and how was she supposed to find that?

Before she'd gone too far, a hand grabbed her arm.

She turned with a gasp.

"It's only me," Professor Haskins said, bringing a finger to his lips. His eyes gleamed with amusement, and he appeared to be holding back a laugh. "Where are you going in such a hurry? Is everything all right?"

"I . . . I was worried that my aunt had sent you running, and so I came after you."

Standing this close to Professor Haskins in the narrow corridor was making her skin prickle with warmth. He smelled nice, like a woodsy soap.

"Are you all right?" she continued because he hadn't spoken. "I—"

"I assure you I am fine, Miss Ballard." His lips twitched.

And it was like the flush of his face transferred to hers, and suddenly she was heated up. "Did you hear my aunt's list?"

His lips twitched again. "I did."

"Did you hear . . . number four?"

His shoulders began to shake, and she realized he was silently laughing. He covered half his face with his hand, keeping his laughter quiet.

Gigi wanted to laugh with him, but that was quite impossible because she was so mortified. "I am so sorry," she whispered.

Professor Haskins continued to laugh quietly, and Gigi covered her own mouth as she felt a smile coming on. She would not laugh. She would not. A small laugh escaped.

"Don't apologize for your aunt," the professor said at last when he had some control again. "I have not laughed this hard in a long time or perhaps ever." He wiped at his eyes.

"You are not mortified?"

"I don't know what I am, but I can assure you this tour will not be like any other I've ever led."

"I can't apologize enough," Gigi said, stepping away and putting more distance between them. "I will speak to my aunt privately. She cannot carry on like this, especially when there are others who can overhear."

"Miss Ballard." Professor Haskins grasped her hand, drawing her to a stop. "Please don't be troubled over this."

She looked down at their hands—his were unexpectedly rough—then back into his hazel eyes that were quite dark in the dim light of the corridor gas lamps. "It's not fair to you."

"I see it as a bit of entertainment," he said. "As long as no one is hurt in the process."

Gigi swallowed. "No, that wouldn't happen."

"Of course not." His gaze held hers for a long moment, broken only when someone else entered the passageway.

Professor Haskins's hand slipped from hers, taking its warmth with him.

"If you are sure?" she asked in a quiet voice.

His smile appeared. "I am sure."

She was grateful that he was being so conciliatory, but what of the days to come? Would he tire quickly of her aunt's persistence?

The passenger, an older man, walked past them with a nod to each of them. After he'd moved down a ways, the professor said, "Remember, we are to be . . . what did you say?"

"Brave, strong, and noble."

He tapped his temple as if committing the words to memory. "Excellent, Miss Ballard." Then he shifted and offered his arm to her. "Shall we?"

She looked down at his arm, then up at him. "Are you sure? If we walk in there together, my aunt will probably faint in her chair."

"I think we have a list to attend to."

The soft low tones of his voice made the pulse at the base of her neck flutter.

"Strong, brave, noble," he whispered.

"Strong, brave, noble," she repeated with a soft laugh.

He grinned, then stepped forward, guiding her. They entered the dining car together, and sure enough, all eyes at her aunt's table widened as they saw Gigi walk in with the professor.

He gallantly escorted her to the table.

Aunt Rowena's mouth gaped as the professor said, "Good evening, ladies. Might I join you for dessert?"

"Of—of course," Aunt Rowena responded.

There was a bit of flurry as the professor added a chair to the table without waiting for the waiter's help. When he sat, all eyes were still trained on him. "Now, Miss Ballard says that you have some questions to ask me."

Aunt Rowena's face went up at least two shades in red, and her gaze cut to Gigi.

But Gigi was speechless at his boldness herself.

"Professor Haskins overheard part of our discussion, so I explained that we have put together a list."

Thankfully Aunt Rowena didn't look upset or dismayed. She looked . . . impressed. She turned a broad smile upon Professor Haskins. "Indeed, we do."

CHAPTER SIX

GIGI HAD NEVER WITNESSED AN interrogation before, but she would guess it was similar to what took place over the next few minutes.

Aunt Rowena was gracious enough to wait for the desserts to be served. And Professor Haskins's dessert was rerouted to their table.

"It is good of you to join us, Professor," Aunt Rowena said after taking a delicate bite of her trifle.

To his credit, the professor turned an inquisitive gaze upon her aunt, as if he had no idea what type of question would be thrown at him. And to Aunt Rowena's credit, she didn't need her list after all to ask her questions.

"We are simply interested in learning more about you." Aunt Rowena's eyes had brightened, and her smile was so innocent that Gigi was almost fooled herself. "Tell us about your family, Professor. We'd love to hear about your wife and children."

Professor Haskins had ordered *crème au caramel*, and he paused before taking a bite. "I am not married, nor do I have any children."

"Ah," Aunt Rowena said.

"Ah," Irene said.

And here it came. "Ah," Blanche said.

Aunt Rowena leaned forward. "You are a bachelor, then?"

Professor Haskins had just popped a bite of *crème au caramel* into his mouth, so everyone took their own bites of dessert as they waited for him to speak again.

"This is a story I do not tell many people," he said in a low tone. He was not looking at Gigi, but she felt as if he were speaking directly to her. "I was engaged a few years ago to a woman who decided that, although she was deeply in love with me, my income was not sufficient for the life she envisioned living."

"Goodness," Aunt Rowena said. "How awful."

Blanche's eyes narrowed as she studied him quite intently. "You are a renowned professor. Surely you can give a woman a comfortable life."

How Professor Haskins wasn't bothered by the bold, and borderline rude, statement was beyond Gigi.

He only looked slightly bemused. "Olivia would not agree with you."

Irene tutted and shook her head as if she were feeling every bit of the distress the professor must have experienced all those years ago.

"We are very sorry," Aunt Rowena said, her tone more brusque now. "I hope you do not hold Olivia's actions against any other women."

"I do not," the professor said as a smile played on his lips. It was a very slight one—one that only Gigi noticed. His gaze shifted to hers, and she didn't miss the warmth in his hazel eyes. In this lighting, his eyes were more green than brown. "But I must say that my heart was broken enough that I declared myself a bachelor from then on."

No one spoke at the table. Not for a long moment.

"But if you met the *right* woman, Professor Haskins," Aunt Rowena finally ventured, "surely you would reconsider."

The professor's gaze slid away from Gigi's. Why did her legs feel watery?

"I suppose one should never say *never*," the professor said.

Aunt Rowena beamed. "Exactly. That is what I say often. Don't I, Georgina?"

"Uh, yes, yes, you do."

The professor's mouth had quirked again, but he didn't look at her, which was probably a good thing since Gigi was feeling rather flushed.

"Where do you live?" Irene blurted out. "That is, if it is no great secret."

"Not at all," the professor said, digging into his dessert and taking another bite. "I live in Bloomsbury, near the University of London."

Gigi realized they were now on question number three. These women were clever, very clever.

"Do you have good neighbors?" Aunt Rowena asked, bringing everything back to center.

"My neighbors are friendly and resourceful."

"And what about your community?" Aunt Rowena continued. "Do you participate in social events?"

Professor Haskins smiled. "When I have time, I'm not opposed to social events."

Aunt Rowena looked relieved. "Excellent."

But Gigi was quite finished with the interrogation of the professor. "Do we have time for a game of whist or is everyone too tired?"

Irene covered her mouth to stifle a yawn. "I am going to retire as soon as my dessert is finished."

"I will too," Blanche said. "We must be well rested for our adventures in Strasbourg tomorrow. Oh, but the two of you should stay and visit. You're both young people, and you certainly have more energy."

"Yes, do stay," Aunt Rowena said, patting Professor Haskins's arm. "I can manage without Georgina tonight." Her smile was bright, making her plans obvious.

It turned out the professor could turn down Aunt Rowena's subtle hints. "I'm afraid I must review my notes for our visit to the *Musée Zoologique*. Although I've been more than once, I like to add in new insights from the last time I was there." He rose before anyone could protest. "Good night, ladies."

Gigi tried not to gaze after him, but she didn't look away in time because he turned his head before disappearing into the next train car, and their gazes connected briefly.

Gigi then noted with surprise that the other members of the tour had already left the dining car, and there was only one other table occupied— by a man dressed all in black. He had a dessert plate sitting untouched in front of him as he perused a newspaper. In his other hand, he held his smokeless pipe.

"Well, the professor is even more eligible than I could have hoped for," Aunt Rowena said in a lowered tone. *Now* she was acting discreet.

"The poor man," Blanche added, "to have his heart broken just because he lives on a professor's salary."

"If that didn't happen though, he wouldn't be available for our Georgina," Aunt Rowena said with a sly smile.

Gigi didn't know what she expected—that her aunt and her aunt's friends would ask the professor questions, then leave the issue alone? No. Now they were even more determined. "I believe Professor Haskins made his case clear," she said. "We should honor his wishes. Besides, I did not come on this tour to be paired up. I'd like to enjoy my time with the three of you."

Blanche smiled. Irene giggled. Aunt Rowena frowned.

"I have a confession to make." Aunt Rowena lifted her chin. "I did quite a bit of research on Professor Haskins before I booked this tour."

It was Gigi's turn to frown.

"Everything he said is true," Aunt Rowena said. "I have already confirmed it, so I am pleased to announce that he has proven himself honest. This was number five on my list. The man my niece marries must be forthright and honest in all his dealings."

Gigi didn't know if she was hearing her aunt correctly. Did this mean Aunt Rowena had planned to match Gigi with the professor from the beginning? Even before the tour? "Aunt . . . I don't understand. I thought you wanted to go on the tour to see the museums. Has this been about matchmaking from the beginning?"

By the flush on her aunt's face, Gigi knew she'd guessed right. She regretted that they had an audience for this conversation. But they were already too far into it, and the other women had been witnesses to everything.

"It is all my fault," her aunt said, her voice trembling with emotion.

"What is all your fault?"

"Jimmy Dorsal."

Gigi went very still. How in the world could anything about Jimmy Dorsal be her aunt's fault? Had they even met? Gigi tried to think back to an event where Aunt Rowena and Jimmy had both attended.

"I . . ." Aunt Rowena began, her face flushing pink. "I overheard a conversation with Mr. Dorsal and another woman. I couldn't see them since they were quite hidden behind one of those large potted plants at the Evans' charity ball. Jimmy was flirting with her."

Gigi blinked. A man flirting with other women at a ball was commonplace enough, especially when said man wasn't engaged or otherwise committed. Yet Jimmy wasn't that type of man—unless he had intentions. Did he have intentions for another woman? Is that why he stopped seeing her?

"I listened for as long as I dared," Aunt Rowena continued in a halting tone. "He was sweet-talking her. Or so I thought."

Gigi's stomach began a slow turn.

"I moved away but kept within sight so I could see when the pair emerged from behind the plant," Aunt Rowena said. "After a few minutes, sure enough, Jimmy left the location. Another minute passed, and the young woman came out too. I'll never forget the red of her hair. She was a pretty thing."

Gigi nodded for her aunt to continue. The sooner this story was told, the better.

Aunt Rowena reached for her nearly empty glass and took a sip. "The night before, you'd told your mother and me that you were keen on Jimmy. You begged to wear that new dress your mother had bought you for Christmas. You wanted to wear it early because you hoped to impress Jimmy."

Now Gigi remembered the night clearly. She'd spent hours getting ready and even let her sister, Lillian, fuss over her, something that typically would have only made her more flustered. Jimmy had asked her to dance early in the evening, and Gigi had felt like she was walking on clouds the next hour. But when she saw him again, he seemed distant. He didn't even look at her when they were in the same conversation with a group of mutual friends. And instead of asking her to dance again, which he'd mentioned when they'd first danced, he'd asked Mary Wright. But Mary wasn't redheaded. She was a dark brunette.

"I remember," Gigi said in a small voice, wondering where her aunt was taking this story.

"I brought Agnes with me to stand close enough to Jimmy so that he could overhear our conversation," Aunt Rowena said. "I said a few things that would turn off any young beau."

Gigi's stomach felt like it had turned inside out. "What did you say?" she whispered.

"I told Agnes, 'Last night, my niece Georgina confessed her devotion to a young man she'd been writing letters to. They've quite fallen in love over the written words between them.'" Aunt Rowena lowered her head, and her shoulders shook.

Was she crying?

Gigi felt like she could barely breathe. The moments ticked by with no one speaking.

Then Aunt Rowena brushed at her cheeks and raised her chin. Sure enough, there were tears in her eyes. "I later found out that the redhead he'd been speaking to was his cousin, and what I'd thought were romantic words were really just words of familial affection." Her voice broke. "I hope you can forgive me, dear Georgina. It wasn't until months later that I realized my mistake, and by then, he'd already announced his engagement to another woman."

Gigi blinked against the stinging in her own eyes. How could this be real? How could this have happened? How could her aunt . . . ?

"Since then, I have searched for a match for you," Aunt Rowena continued. "But there has been one failure after another."

"What do you mean?" Gigi dreaded the answer.

Aunt Rowena exhaled slowly. "The men who have paid you suit over the past year—Richard Turley, Phillip Brandon, and Reggie Mann."

CHAPTER SEVEN

Dear Lillian,

We have settled in Strasbourg for two days. The city is quaint yet metropolitan, and homes along the Ill river are charming and colorful. I feel as if I'm in a completely different world. So much has happened since I've last written, and it hasn't even been twenty-four hours. First, Aunt Rowena has made a list to get to know the professor better. Let me back up though. He knows all about Aunt Rowena's matchmaking intentions, and we've had quite a laugh over it. We're in cahoots together, you might say. But there is more. Last night, Aunt Rowena confessed to her role in turning Jimmy Dorsal away from me . . .

STRASBOURG WAS A BEAUTIFUL CITY. As Gigi walked at the back of the tour group, she marveled at the colorful homes and clean cobblestone streets. They were walking to the *Musée Zoologique*, and then the professor would take them to some famous restaurant. She also noted the clothing that people wore, looking for inspiration. She loved the tidy hats and the heeled shoes worn by the women. The women also wore a lot more lace and ruffles at the neck. Interesting.

Up ahead, the professor was giving a few tidbits to Blanche, who seemed enthralled with his every word. He hadn't spoken directly to Gigi, except for a standard greeting when they'd been surrounded by the rest of the group.

Her mind shifted from her fashion watch to the story he'd told of his broken engagement. Although he seemed quite recovered from the ordeal, his ego must have been broken enough that he'd declared himself a lifelong bachelor. Had he loved his fiancée so deeply? Gigi's curiosity was not because she thought of him as a potential suitor. No, her curiosity was because she wondered if perhaps Jimmy Dorsal had been heartbroken over *her*.

It was far in the past now, and although Gigi had been stunned at her aunt's confession, Gigi also understood the mistake, as terrible as it had been. And those other men that Aunt Rowena had apparently sent Gigi's way?

Thankfully, the beauty and distance of Strasbourg helped Gigi not feel so weighted down by her cycling thoughts and questions. As far as she knew, Jimmy and Mary were happy together, and it would do no good for Gigi to harbor regrets or anger now. She assumed this on an intellectual level, but the aching in her heart had persisted all night.

"Are you all right, Georgina?" Blanche asked, moving close and linking arms. The woman was decked out in rubies today. How much jewelry could one person bring on a train?

"I am fine," Gigi said quickly. "Sleeping in a new place each night is not exactly easy. But this trip is worth every discomfort."

"I agree," Blanche said, but her brows pinched as she focused on Gigi. "Are you quite upset with your aunt?"

"I was surprised. That's all." Gigi suspected that Aunt Rowena could overhear them since she was not too far ahead, walking with Irene. Besides, the tears shed last night were enough. It was time to move on. For everyone.

"Yes, we all were," Blanche soothed. "It certainly demonstrates how a single misunderstanding can muddy things up."

To say the least . . .

"This is why you need to give the professor a chance," Blanche said, thankfully lowering her voice this time.

Gigi went silent. Now that she knew how much Aunt Rowena had orchestrated coming on this tour—and how sorry she was for everything— and how she was trying to make it up to Gigi . . . It was still overwhelming, and she would need to have a conversation with the professor. This was no longer a silly game they could laugh about in the dim corridor of a train. Her aunt had quite fixated on him and taken things to the extreme.

"Ah, here we are," Professor Haskins said up ahead.

The tour members gathered around him as he stood in front of the ornate three-story building. "This museum was built in the early 1700s based upon Jean Hermann's Gallery of Natural History. Inside, you will see an impressive collection of insects, birds, mammals, and marine invertebrates. Included are fish and reptiles, as well as animals that are extinct. Now this is not the typical art museum you might have expected to visit on our tour," the professor said. "But you will see how these collections are art in and of themselves."

"Goodness," Blanche murmured. "So many dead things."

Gigi suppressed a smile.

Inside the museum, Blanche was proven one hundred percent correct. At first the group stayed together, but after the first hour, the two couples had split off, and Aunt Rowena and her friends were taking extra time in the room with polar bears and walruses. Gigi was impatient to move on, so she soon found herself in the area with several African animals.

"The giraffe is magnificent. Don't you think?" a male voice spoke behind her.

Gigi didn't need to turn to know that it was Professor Haskins. "Quite remarkable." The elegant animal stood several feet taller than Gigi, and if she'd been at some distance, she might have believed the giraffe to be alive. She heard the professor's steps grow closer, and from her peripheral vision, she saw him stop a few feet away from her.

She peeked at him as he looked up the length of the giraffe. The professor was a fine-looking man, she decided, but his patience was more impressive. He'd done the right thing in telling her aunt that he was a confirmed bachelor, because if he'd been open to a relationship, then Gigi might have developed a small attachment to him.

She looked away before he could catch her gazing at him.

"It would be interesting to spend one's life exploring and collecting natural history specimens," he said. "Don't you think so?"

"Indeed," she said. "It would also be exciting to discover a new type of animal or insect."

"I agree."

She felt his gaze upon her. Looking over at him, she offered a half smile. "Are you interested in insect collecting?"

"Not particularly, but I do find it fascinating." He slipped his hands into his trouser pockets. "How about you?"

"I'll pass."

He chuckled, his hazel eyes warm and light, and her pulse went up a notch. "You know, you shouldn't be so worried about the lists your aunt is making. I understand how some people get caught up in the business of matchmaking."

Should she tell him? "It's more than that . . ." She took a breath, listening for any sounds of other tour members coming into this same display room.

Professor Haskins took a step closer, and one of his brows quirked. "Don't tell me she's added to her list."

"Not exactly," Gigi said. "It appears that we are on this tour because she has researched *you* in particular."

This surprised him, she could tell. Would it upset him too?

"I'm so embarrassed to say this because my aunt is a dear but sometimes misguided woman," Gigi said. "I hope that you will still find humor in this after I tell you, and please know I found out only last night in a tearful confession."

Now he was frowning. "What's happened?" He looked truly concerned, but Gigi was afraid that would be changing in a moment.

She told him everything. How her aunt had arranged this trip specifically so that Gigi would meet the professor—who her aunt had inquired about beforehand to make sure he met her approval.

Gigi told him how she'd been attached to a man named Jimmy Dorsal and how her aunt had misread so many things. And she told him about the consequences that followed, including the other men who had attempted to court her. When Gigi finished relaying the details, she felt like she'd been pulled along on a bumpy wagon ride. Everything inside of her felt shaken. More so than last night. Maybe it was because she hadn't fully processed it until speaking of the events aloud.

"Miss Ballard," Professor Haskins said in a soft voice. "I'm very sorry."

It was then she realized that tears were falling down her cheeks. She brushed at them, mortified that she'd cried in front of this man.

But the professor only moved closer and held out a handkerchief.

Gigi took it and pressed at her damp cheeks. "I'm sorry for laying so much upon you. I guess I am more affected than I realized."

His hand rested on her upper arm. "It is a lot to deal with."

Gigi folded the handkerchief, then pressed the backside to her cheeks again because the tears were still coming. "It's all in the past, except for one thing: you. I can't bear to think that now we've put you in this uncomfortable situation."

The professor squeezed her arm lightly, then dropped his hand. "Why don't you let me talk to your aunt, and I will clear a few things up."

This made Gigi feel even worse. "I've already spoken to her. She's promised she's given up her agenda."

"Well then," he began, "there's no reason to add in more distress."

Gigi nodded her gratitude. "I feel like I am either apologizing or thanking you every time I see you."

The professor's smile was soft, and their gazes clung for a moment. Gigi's pulse began its upward climb again.

"You are a good niece to your aunt," he said. "That is clear, and she is fortunate to have such a forgiving relative."

Gigi sighed. "I suppose. Thank you . . . again." Her smile peeked through, despite her recent tears.

He chuckled. "You're welcome—for whatever you're thanking me for. I have been remiss though, and I should find you refreshment and a place to sit and recover."

No one had entered the display room they were in, but that could change at any moment.

"I will be fine," Gigi insisted. "I'm not often given over to hysterics, so you are an unfortunate man to witness this one."

He tilted his head, studying her closely. And what did he see? Her tear-stained face? And probably a reddened nose. "Did you love him?"

Gigi went still. She knew what he was asking and who he was referring to.

"At the time I thought I did," she said in a hesitant voice. "Now, looking back, I know that perhaps I cared more for him than he did me. He moved on remarkably quickly, without a backward glance, it seems. We weren't engaged though, so perhaps things were more in my head than what was real between us."

The professor only nodded.

"And you?" she asked. He'd brought up her lost love, so perhaps it was all right for her to bring up his lost love too.

The professor turned toward the wildlife display again. Clasping his hands behind his back, he seemed to be in deep thought.

For a moment, Gigi wondered if she'd crossed an invisible line or had offended him. A broken engagement was more of a serious event than what she'd gone through.

Then he said, "I trusted her. I think that was the most painful part. Yes, I loved her, and I believed she loved me. But the trust was the thing that should have held us together above all else."

His words were so melancholy that Gigi almost handed him back his handkerchief, but it was quite damp with her own tears. Besides, he wasn't exactly tearful. His voice sounded rough around the edges, as if the time

that had passed since his broken engagement had been much shorter than
a few years.

"I'm sorry about the broken trust," Gigi said. "I can't imagine how hard
it would be to go through that."

"You're apologizing again." His gaze shifted to her, and she was gratified
to see the light back in his eyes.

"I suppose I am." She gave him a small smile.

And he returned it.

"Now, Miss Ballard," he said, extending his arm. "How would you like
to see the Jean Hermann collection?"

Gigi slipped her hand around the crook of his elbow and inhaled the
woodsy scent she was becoming so familiar with. "I'd love to. Lead the way,
Professor Haskins."

CHAPTER EIGHT

Dear Lillian,

I hope I'm not boring you with all this talk of Professor Haskins, but he is proving to be the most fascinating and knowledgeable person I've ever known. He seems to know a little bit about everything. Yesterday we visited the Zoological Museum, and today we went to Notre-Dame and its museum as well. In addition to listening to his lectures, I had more than one conversation with Professor Haskins, and he is not bothered by Aunt Rowena's grand matchmaking plan. It is only an amusement to him, which bespeaks of his good nature and unending patience. No wonder these tour members in their "twilight" years enjoy him so much.

Now, I know what you're thinking, and you can erase that from your mind completely. I'm not about to fall in love or do anything foolish when it comes to Professor Haskins. He is only a friend, and we both have quite agreed that's all we'll ever be. He has his past, you see, and he says he cannot give away a heart that has been broken in half. Yes, he is a bit of a poet. Another attribute I quite admire . . .

"WE MEET AGAIN," A DEEP voice said, pulling Gigi from her concentration. "You have returned to zeh Orient Express, I see."

She looked up from her notebook, upon which she'd been sketching a daring design—one of a lady's jacket with a brooch made from a mounted dragonfly. They'd boarded the Orient Express again and were now on their way to Munich. The dining car was mostly empty following the supper hour, with only a few occupants who were having a late tea. Aunt Rowena and her friends had already retired for the evening.

The man in all black stood near her table. *Nicholas.* He wore a hat, as if he'd just come in from outside, and he held his smokeless pipe in one hand.

Professor Haskins had told her little about this man named Nicholas, and she was surprised to see him yet again. Because the professor hadn't raised any alarm, she supposed she shouldn't shy away from speaking with him.

"How are you, sir?" she said out of both politeness and curiosity.

"I am vell." He nodded to the seat across from her, and she nodded back. He sat with a flourish, but a distance had appeared in his dark eyes as if he weren't really seeing her.

She didn't know what to make of him or how this was the second time they were in a conversation without any formal introduction. "I am Georgina Ballard."

He took a puff on his pipe, although no smoke came out. "Nicholas."

Ah. So their small talk was to be very small talk. She looked down at her notepad and the sketch that had taken form there.

"You add sorrow to zeh art on your pages."

Gigi looked up again at Nicholas. "This is not art."

His thick brows pulled. "You are creating something new, no?"

Her gaze flitted to her sketch. "Yes . . ."

"Zis is zeh definition of art, Miss Ballard."

Something in her chest expanded. She'd never considered herself an artist, and yet . . . perhaps Nicholas was right.

He took another drag on his pipe, and although there was no smoke, she thought she detected the scent of French baguettes, reminding her of Strasbourg.

"You are troubled, I see," he continued unprompted. "You must remember zaht art is one way to work out zeh heart's grief."

Gigi blinked as she felt a slight tremble in her fingers. Was he implying that she still had a broken heart and somehow she could work through it by sketching?

Abruptly he stood, and she drew back a little, surprised at his brusque action.

"Have a good evening, Miss Ballard." He checked his pocket watch, then tipped his hat and strode off before she could reply in kind or ask him for clarification.

She stared after him for a moment, wondering what the man was about. Where was he from and where was he headed? What type of occupation did he have?

A waiter appeared and changed her cup for a new one of steaming tea. She thanked him, then tried to concentrate again on her sketching. She turned the page and began a new design, drawing another ladies' shirtwaist. She made it tailored but with a gaping hole in the sleeve. After considering it for a moment, she drew over it to make it look as good as new again.

She felt oddly satisfied.

"How is your German, Miss Ballard?" someone said.

She knew it was Professor Haskins before she looked up, and her breathing felt a bit faint by the time their gazes connected.

"I know a few words," Gigi said, trying not to smile too broadly.

"Ah, ones such as *how are you* and *thank you very much*."

"Precisely." Their smiles caught, and Gigi was the one to look away first.

"Do you mind?" the professor asked, motioning to the seat across from hers, just as Nicholas had moments before.

"Of course not." She wanted to grin. "You missed Nicholas . . . The man with the pipe?"

"He is on board again?" the professor mused. "I'm sure I'll see him soon enough then."

He turned his attention to the window. The dark landscape was brightened by the silvery moonlight.

Gigi peeked at his profile. The gas lamps of the lounge car played upon his features. She'd become well-acquainted with the angle of his jaw, the slope of his nose, his dark brows, his amused hazel eyes, and of course, the waves of his pale blond hair. He was a striking man, and if his heart wasn't so closed, she had no doubt he would have been snatched up long ago.

He turned his head toward her, the edge of a smile on his lips. She looked down quickly, willing her face not to flush.

"What are you sketching this evening, Miss Ballard?"

"Oh." She closed the notebook. "A few ladies' jacket designs."

The professor extended his hand. "May I see your designs?"

Truthfully, Gigi had shown very few people outside her family circle her designs. And never a man. Not even Nicholas had seemed to peer at her sketches when he was sitting across from her.

"Are they top secret?" the professor asked, amusement in his tone. "Or perhaps scandalous in nature?"

Gigi laughed. "They're not scandalous, I assure you. Quite proper, in fact." She slid the notebook toward him.

Professor Haskins took his time in perusing the pages. He only nodded a few times, but there was no other reaction, either favorable or otherwise as he examined each design. Some he only looked at for a handful of seconds. For others, he angled the notebook and took more time studying.

"Well." He closed the notebook and handed it back. "Why did you not tell me you're an artist?"

The second man in so many minutes to reference artistry. Gigi didn't know what to make of it. She accepted the notebook. "I'm not sure that designing ladies' clothing is considered art."

"On the contrary, Miss Ballard," the professor said, a smile in his voice. "Think of the paintings and sculptures we have viewed thus far. What are they comprised of?"

"Most of them have been men or women in various poses or activities."

"Yes." The professor leaned back in his seat. "And what is the artist doing as he creates these pieces?"

Gigi was stumped. What answer was he seeking?

"Art is the study of the human form physically and the study of the human mind mentally and emotionally. Do you think if the Mona Lisa were in the nude or David were clothed that would change the nature of the works?"

Gigi's brows shot up. "Definitely."

"You're correct," he said. "So, how can creating that clothing from scratch not be considered art as well?"

Gigi opened her mouth, then closed it. He certainly had a way with logic. "All right, then. If you insist, I'll consider my designs art."

He chuckled. "I insist."

She was smiling, and her chest felt airy.

"Have you ever considered men's fashions?"

Gigi lifted a shoulder in a shrug. "Not exactly."

The professor motioned to his jacket. "What embellishments would you give a jacket like this?"

She tilted her head, enjoying this moment of being able to openly study him. His jacket was a deep brown, and it set off his blond hair and deepened his hazel eyes. Perfect, really. But she couldn't tell him that. She had to find a way to improve the article of clothing.

"I'd add a second pocket so that there is one on each side of the jacket, then . . ." She paused. "Change the buttons to navy. You could pair the jacket with navy trousers to bring out the color more."

Professor Haskins leaned forward. "Impressive. Can you do it? I can go change and bring it back to you."

Gigi drew back. "You want me to alter your jacket?"

His smile was bright. "Sure."

She could only stare, and then she laughed. "I don't think so. I mean, what would my aunt say? Me altering your clothing sounds like a—"

"Wifely thing to do?" His teasing grin made her skin prickle.

"Yes."

"Or a business woman's project? I will pay you just as I'd pay a tailor."

"Don't pay me," Gigi said immediately. "And I am no tailor . . . I'm a dressmaker. Men's clothing is different."

One of his dark brows rose, but his eyes danced with merriment. "How so, Miss Ballard? Men's clothing has pleats, darts, sleeves, lapels, lace, ruffles, and that's just the top half—"

"All right, stop," Gigi said, holding up a hand. The last thing she needed him to do was describe parts of a trouser or men's underthings. "I will alter your jacket, but you are not to pay me."

His eyes crinkled at the corners. "I'll be back in a minute."

And before she could respond, he rose from his seat and strode out of the dining car.

"Well," Gigi muttered to herself. She couldn't very well be taking the man's jacket off his hands when there were a few people still in the dining car. No one she knew, but she didn't want Aunt Rowena to hear about this from someone else.

So she left the dining car herself and waited in the corridor of the sleeping car where the members of the tour were staying. She didn't have to wait long, and when he came out of one of the compartments at the end of the corridor, her heart involuntarily skipped a beat. He'd removed his tie, and that left his collar open at the top.

The dim corridor lighting made his hair darker, more golden, and his eyes nearly black.

"Is this a covert exchange?" he asked, his tone low and warm.

"It is."

"Very well," he said. "Here is the top-secret jacket, and we will rendezvous later when it is finished."

"Very well," she repeated, trying not to smirk. She took the jacket from his outstretched hand, and for the briefest moment, their fingers brushed.

Like before, she noticed his were warm and rougher than she'd expect for a man she thought spent a lot of time inside a university. Maybe he had outdoor hobbies or pursuits.

She draped the jacket over her arm. The weight of it felt like a connection to the man it belonged to. And then everything seemed to go still between them. She was keenly aware that they were standing together in a narrow corridor. The soft lighting, the draw of the man before her, and his woodsy soap scent all made her feel as if she'd stepped into another world.

And that would not do because now she was thinking about what it might be like if he took her hand, if their fingers intertwined, if he leaned close . . .

She sidestepped him. "Well, good night, Professor Haskins. I'll see you in Munich."

He turned to watch her go, and as it happened, she had to pass quite close to him.

Their arms didn't brush, their hands didn't touch, and that was a relief. And a disappointment. Gigi must be tired and fanciful. That was all. She and the professor were moving forward into a lovely friendship, and yet her mind was trying to twist things unfairly. Surely, he wouldn't be so courteous and charming and friendly if he thought she was thinking of him in a new light now. She should walk quickly and disappear inside her berth, where at last she'd be able to take a full breath.

"Good night, Miss Ballard," the professor murmured.

She continued along the corridor, not daring to look back. She could already feel his gaze upon her, and she told herself firmly that he was being a gentleman and making sure she got to her berth without incident. What incident, she didn't know. It was just something to keep her mind focused.

He'd paid her a high compliment in asking her to alter his jacket. And she'd do it for free because they were friends. Friends. That was all. And that was how it would remain.

CHAPTER NINE

Dear Lillian,

I think I've quite fallen in love. Now before you fall over in shock, it is not what you think. I've fallen in love with the city of Munich. If only I'd paid more attention in my short stint in German lessons, then I'd inquire at the dressmaker shops and see if they are hiring.

I'm teasing of course, but oh, how beautiful this place is. In about an hour, we will join the tour and visit the Kunstareal— the museum quarter in the center of Munich. Professor Haskins has promised us that we'll see many of the old masters. I'm so looking forward to it. You might also be interested to know that I'm working on an alteration of the professor's jacket. It seems he's quite enthusiastic for me to rearrange his fashion . . .

THE ELEGANT SPIRES OF THE towering buildings left Gigi in awe as the tour traveled by horse and carriage along the streets of Munich. The day was cool and overcast—unseasonably so—but that didn't dampen Gigi's spirits in the least.

Aunt Rowena was also in cheerful form.

By unspoken agreement, they'd dropped the topic of Aunt Rowena's past interference, and she'd quite agreed upon dropping all designs of uniting the professor with Gigi. So now, when Aunt Rowena addressed the professor with some questions, Gigi no longer worried there was an ulterior motive behind them.

"The focus of the Neue Pinakothek Museum is European art of the eighteenth and nineteenth century, which makes it one of the most important museums of nineteenth-century art in the world," the professor was telling Irene, who sat on the bench across from them. The members of the tour were in two groups, and the whist club happened to have the professor in their carriage this time around.

"I can't even pronounce any of these streets," Irene said with a light giggle. "They're all in German."

"I am quite proficient," Blanche interjected. She opened up a brochure she'd snagged from the hotel and began to read. "*Das Kunstareal in München zählt mit seinen weltberühmten Museen zu den wichtigsten Kunst-und Kulturzentren Europas.*"

"Oh, you always have to outdo everyone," Irene said, her voice borderline cross.

"But no one speaks *French* as well as you, Irene," Aunt Rowena hurried to say.

"Well, thank you." Irene gave the professor an obvious wink.

Gigi wanted to groan, but Professor Haskins seemed to take everything in stride. He also effectively steered the conversation back to the museums they were about to visit. His gaze flitted to Gigi's from time to time, and she tried not to react to their shared glances. But it was impossible not to, which made her grateful for the cooler weather to stave off any threatening blushes.

They were friends, only friends, but it was still a wonderful thing. Something she hoped never to get used to or take for granted.

As for the others . . . it was remarkable, really, what the presence of a handsome young gentleman did for the demeanor of a group of older women. Gigi knew she must count herself in the affected group because, yes, she also felt more lively when the professor was near.

Gigi hadn't started on his jacket, and she would wait until Aunt Rowena had retired to bed tonight so that there wouldn't be any speculation on her part.

"Goodness, would you look at that," Aunt Rowena said, motioning with her gloved hand toward the museum square.

They'd turned onto a road leading to a series of stoic, rectangular buildings. A massive green lawn connected the buildings, making the museums appear even grander in appearance.

"Is that it, Professor?" Irene asked, grasping his arm.

"That is the place," Professor Haskins said. "We could spend two full days here, but alas, we'll have only one."

Gigi gazed at the rows of windows of the Neue Pinakothek as they approached. The carriages finally slowed. Professor Haskins climbed out of their carriage first, then helped each woman down, one by one. Once Aunt Rowena was safely on her feet, Gigi handed the cane to the professor, and he gave it over to her aunt.

Gigi was the last to exit the carriage, and although she'd already steeled herself for grasping the professor's hand as an anchor to climb out, she wasn't prepared for the fluttering in her stomach at the physical contact. *Enough*, she told herself.

Outwardly, she smiled and released her hold the moment both her feet were on the ground.

But the professor didn't step away at first.

"How are you this morning, Miss Ballard?" he asked in a lowered tone.

It was a casual question, one he might have asked in front of an entire group of people. But he hadn't. He'd waited until they were separated from the others, who were now congregating together, so it felt more personal.

"I haven't lost a shoe, and my hair has stayed in place."

Professor Haskins chuckled. "You are never predictable. How can that be?"

She smiled up at him, even though she was in very grave danger of exposing how much she enjoyed his company. "And how are you, Professor Haskins?"

"I am looking forward to visiting some of my favorite museums and no longer worrying over your aunt's list."

Gigi tilted her head. "You are relieved then?"

"Most relieved." His gaze held hers. "Because I do not like to establish relationships on manufactured lists."

"How do you establish relationships then?" she asked. "I'm merely curious in case my aunt asks."

His mouth curved into a smile, but before he could answer, someone called out.

"Professor Haskins, are you giving away museum secrets to only Miss Ballard?" It was Blanche.

Gigi was confident that comment had caught her aunt's attention. Sure enough, her aunt had turned to look over at them, and her brows were nearly to her hairline.

"Of course not," the professor said quickly. "My museum secrets are for all to know." He strode toward the other women.

Gigi followed, making sure her aunt was doing all right. She'd complained of being out of breath and her legs feeling sore this morning, and Gigi had hoped the carriage ride would alleviate the soreness before they were on their feet once again in the museum.

"How are you feeling?" Gigi asked her aunt when she caught up to her and linked arms to give her aunt added support.

"Well enough." Aunt Rowena cast her a sideways glance. "The professor sure smiles at you a lot."

Gigi hoped to high heaven that Professor Haskins hadn't overheard.

"We are friends, Aunt Rowena. That is all," she said.

"The best relationships start with friendship," her aunt mused.

"I've no doubt," Gigi said. "And some relationships are best to remain as friendships. Don't you agree?"

Aunt Rowena knew she couldn't argue. "You are right. I should not be reading into a shared smile or a friendly conversation between the two of you. I have already made too many mistakes in this regard, and I'm determined to let you manage your life, dear Georgina."

Gigi had heard this same sentiment the night before and could only hope that her aunt would stick to it. It was nice to know that her aunt cared so deeply for her, but would she be able to stick to it?

Gigi wasn't sure if there was a pebble or something else in the lane as they walked the last few steps to the museum, but suddenly her aunt pitched forward.

Gigi reacted immediately but was only able to prevent her aunt from falling completely over.

Finding herself on her knees, holding her aunt up, surprised her as much as it seemed to have surprised Aunt Rowena.

"Are you all right?" Gigi said.

"I—I don't know," her aunt said, then moaned. "My ankle. I think I've twisted it."

Gigi shifted again and wrapped an arm about her aunt's waist to give her more support. "Let's find a place to sit inside. Then we can examine the damage."

Since Gigi and her aunt had been at the back of the group, the others didn't immediately notice. But soon, they were surrounded by the entire tour group, who fussed and fretted over Aunt Rowena. Still clinging to Gigi, Aunt Rowena said, "I need to find a bench. Everyone make way."

Well, her aunt could be decisive even when so recently injured.

Professor Haskins supported her on her other side. "I can carry you if you'd like," he offered.

"Never you mind," Aunt Rowena said. "I don't want to be fussed over."

But she looked right pleased to be fussed over, and Gigi hid a smile as she helped the hobbling woman into the museum. They sat on a bench near the main lobby, and Gigi knelt before her aunt to check her ankle and foot.

The professor knelt right next to her as if doing his own examination. There was not much Gigi could conclude without the knowledge of a doctor, and the professor looked equally perplexed.

"Shall I fetch a doctor?" he asked.

"Nonsense," Aunt Rowena said. "The pain has diminished already. I am perfectly content to sit here."

Gigi readjusted her aunt's skirts as the professor rose. He extended his hand to help her up, and Gigi took it. Now wasn't the time to think upon the feel of his hand against hers.

She settled next to her aunt upon the bench. "I'll wait with you."

"You cannot miss the artwork," Aunt Rowena protested.

"I don't want you left alone in case you need something," Gigi said.

The professor hadn't left their side and seemed intent on hovering. "I've been through the Neue Pinakothek more than once. I'm happy to sit with you, and Miss Ballard can accompany the others."

"Certainly not," Aunt Rowena said. "You are the tour director."

He looked from Aunt Rowena to Gigi, as if he were at a loss for additional ideas.

"I will be fine right here," Gigi said. "I assure both of you." She offered a cheerful smile, hoping to convince the professor further.

"We will take turns," Irene said.

"Yes," Blanche agreed. "We will return shortly and tell you which rooms to visit."

"All right," Gigi said. "That's an excellent plan." She could feel the professor's gaze upon her, and she simply nodded for him to join the tour members.

He hesitated, then said, "Alert a staff member if you need my help with anything."

"We will. Thank you, Professor," Aunt Rowena said with a flick of her hand.

Once the tour group had moved on, Aunt Rowena closed her eyes with a sigh.

"Are you sure I can't call for a doctor?" Gigi asked in a soft voice.

"I am sure," Aunt Rowena said. "I didn't sleep well last night, and that likely added to my clumsiness." She kept her eyes closed, so Gigi let her have her peace.

Surprisingly enough, her aunt did indeed nod off.

So Gigi was left to watch the comings and goings of the museum lobby. The time passed slowly, and Gigi gave up on trying to decipher the various languages spoken around her by other museum guests.

Eventually, Irene showed up with the professor.

Aunt Rowena stirred awake as Irene began to talk. "The professor will take you on a shortened tour, and I'll sit with Rowena. Blanche is still with the others."

Gigi hesitated, but her aunt said, "Go, dear. I'll be fine with Irene."

So Gigi joined the professor, feeling like she was neglecting her duty and feeling a bit warm to have this time alone with the professor even though they were in a museum full of other people.

"I found out why you looked familiar when we first met," the professor said in a low tone as they arrived at a display of paintings.

Gigi glanced at him. "Oh?"

"Yes. It seems you have a look-alike." He smiled and tilted his head. "Come this way."

She walked with him into another room. Large oil paintings in ornate frames graced the walls. The painter seemed familiar. "Is this Johann Friedrich Overbeck?"

"Correct," the professor said. He motioned toward one of the larger paintings of a young woman.

Gigi studied the painting. The woman seemed younger than Gigi, but their brown hair color was identical, as was the shape of their brown eyes. It was uncanny, really. Gigi's lips were fuller and her jaw more angular, but there was a resemblance. Even Gigi could see it. The woman was sitting near a tree in front of a field, her chin resting on her hand.

She read the placard. *Portrait of Vittoria Caldoni, 1821, by Johann Friedrich Overbeck, 1789–1869.*

"You think I resemble this Vittoria Caldoni woman?"

The professor didn't look at her, for his gaze was upon the painting. "There's no doubt. The differences are small. It's almost as if Overbeck used you for the model."

"Which is impossible since this was painted in . . ." She peered at the plaque with the dates. "1821."

The professor turned slowly to face her, his hazel gaze light, warm. "Perhaps he time-traveled?"

She laughed and nudged him. He only grinned. And then they both returned their gazes to the painting.

Neither of them spoke for a while, not until Professor Haskins said, "This has always been a favorite painting of mine. The story behind it is quite remarkable as well."

"Oh?"

"Vittoria Caldoni was fifteen and was one of the most famous Italian models of her time. The Crown Prince Ludwig of Bavaria commissioned the painting, but the work had a mixed reception in the royal court in Munich. For you see, there is added meaning. Vittoria was the daughter of a vineyard keeper, yet in this painting, she also represents a worker in the wheat fields. What does that remind you of?"

"I can't say," Gigi replied.

"It was speculated that Overbeck created a Christian allegory and portrayed Ruth as sitting at the foot of this tree as a figure of the coming generations of Christ."

"Because Christ came through her line."

"Correct."

Goose pimples trailed along her arms as Gigi gazed anew at the painting with greater appreciation. Overbeck had made his subject quite lovely, and there was a serene quality to her somber expression. A slow warmth was spreading through Gigi's body as she thought of how the professor had declared this painting reminded him of her.

In order to break the headiness she was beginning to feel, she said, "Now we must find your look-alike."

"You mean *doppelgänger*? We are in Munich, you know."

Her eyes connected with his. "Right. The doppelgänger of Professor Haskins."

"Clyde."

She blinked.

"It's my name: Clyde Haskins. It sounds odd finding a doppelgänger of Professor Haskins." He winked. "Clyde Haskins seems more personal."

"Well then." Gigi was absolutely breathless, and she hadn't taken one step. "Professor Clyde Haskins it is."

He chuckled. "Where should we start?" He extended his arm for her to take, which was totally unnecessary of him, since the floor was perfectly even, but it was gentlemanly all the same.

"You tell me, Professor," she said, slipping her hand around the crook of his arm. "You're the expert here."

But he didn't start walking yet. He looked down at her, his gaze assessing. "Don't you think we know each other well enough to use first names?"

His smile was teasing, as was his tone.

"What will my aunt think of that?" she mused. "Besides, I don't want the tour members to assume I'm getting special privileges."

Instead of laughing like she thought he would, he drew her a tad closer. "We wouldn't want that. No, indeed," he said in a quiet voice that shivered warm along her back.

CHAPTER TEN

Dear Lillian,

Aunt Rowena will be perfectly fine, but I'm sure she's already written to Mother all about spraining her ankle in Munich. Professor Haskins was very obliging and called in a doctor when we returned to the hotel. The doctor pronounced in his very formal way that Aunt Rowena was to stay off of it for an entire week. The moment he left, Aunt Rowena said she'd never met a more stuffy man in her life, and although she might rest her ankle as frequently as possible, she would not miss out on the tour.

In other news, I spent a good hour with the professor walking through some of the art rooms at Neue Pinakothek. All of them were delightful and amazing. He even compared me to the Vittoria Caldoni painting by Johann Friedrich Overbeck. I was stunned, but I can see the resemblance. Although Vittoria Caldoni is depicted as a much more lovely person. Upon consideration, I don't think a man has ever given me such an extravagant compliment before. He asked me to call him Clyde, as a friend. And of course I rejected that notion. Yes, we are friends, but calling him by his first name somehow seems too personal . . .

"Oh, stop fussing," Aunt Rowena said. "One more hand, and then I'll go and rest."

They were on their way to Vienna, and the game of whist had been going on for nearly two hours. Gigi was tired herself. But she wasn't going to say so around women who were several decades her senior. She'd rather return to the berth and lose herself in her sketchbook. She'd been working on a series of long coats to wear with winter evening gowns.

"Well, I'm going to rest," Irene declared.

"Me too," Blanche added.

"Then we'll find another partner," Aunt Rowena declared in a pinched tone.

She had not been in the best of moods, and Gigi attributed it to the fact that she was pretending her ankle hadn't been sprained. Instead, she was doing too much too soon. "Good evening, sirs," Aunt Rowena said, turning to look at the gentlemen at another table. The professor was wearing his altered jacket tonight, and every time Gigi had caught sight of him, she felt a smile pressing through.

"Would you care to join us in a game of whist?" Aunt Rowena continued.

Gigi bit back her protest. Nicholas and Professor Haskins seemed to be in a deep conversation, but there was no ignoring Aunt Rowena.

Both men looked over.

"Vhist?" Nicholas said. "I would be happy to make an attempt. I don't profess much skill in playing zeh game."

Aunt Rowena only smiled. "Surely a man who knows as many languages as you will have no trouble."

Nicholas's dark brow arched, and Gigi knew he was intrigued.

And how did her aunt know how many languages the man spoke?

"What about you, Professor?" Aunt Rowena persisted. "We need four to make teams of two."

"Very well," the professor said.

"Come sit by me," Aunt Rowena told Gigi, patting the seat next to her.

Gigi obliged, and the two men sat across from them. The professor was directly across from Gigi. In order to save her own blushes, she should try not to meet his gaze too much.

Aunt Rowena gave Nicholas a quick explanation of the game, and once they were through one hand, she declared, "You're a natural, sir."

Nicholas tilted his head, then brought his pipe to his mouth and inhaled. Then exhaled. No smoke came out, but Gigi was almost certain she could smell the scent of German pastries coming from the pipe.

"Tell us about yourself, sir," Aunt Rowena said. "Are you a tradesman? A businessman?"

"International business," Nicholas said.

"Ah, your many languages surely help with your business dealings."

"You are correct, madam. Zeh study of languages has aided me greatly."

Aunt Rowena dealt a second hand of thirteen cards each. "You travel a lot, I assume," she continued. "And what of your family? Do they miss you as you travel?"

"Alas, I have no family," Nicholas said, picking up his cards and deftly organizing them.

Aunt Rowena stilled. "Goodness. I am sorry for that."

"I have learned to find gratitude in other things." His gaze shifted to Gigi. "I may be alone, but I have found my own peace."

Gigi's throat tightened. His words were somber, and she was sure that no one could ever truly see the depths of his dark eyes.

"Yet, I would still caution anyone to choose a different path zhan I did." Nicholas set down a trump card to win the round.

Which path was he speaking about? Gigi wondered.

"Hold your loved ones close. Always." He began the next round with a jack of hearts, and the game progressed.

Gigi glanced at Professor Haskins, and their gazes held for a moment. What had he thought of Nicholas's words? Was he now remembering his own regrets?

"I have one great love in my life," Aunt Rowena said.

Gigi wondered if her aunt was going to name her husband. There had been no children from their union, and he'd left her a wealthy widow. Soon after, she'd reverted to her maiden name, though, a story Gigi had always wondered about.

"Charles and I talked of getting engaged before the Crimean War, then marrying after," Aunt Rowena said.

Charles? Aunt Rowena's late husband was named William . . .

"He never made it home." Aunt Rowena's voice trembled, but she continued on without any tears. "I don't know if I put Charles on a pedestal or what, but no one else ever measured up to him. I did marry eventually, and I hoped that my compatibility with William would turn into love, but William didn't live long enough for me to find out. It is why I reverted back to my maiden name."

"Ah, I am sorry for zeh loss of both Charles and William," Nicholas said.

Aunt Rowena nodded, then took a steadying breath. "One more game?"

Everyone nodded, and she dealt the cards.

By the time the game came to a close, Gigi could no longer hide the yawns that seemed determined to come. Surely her aunt was exhausted too.

"Ve vill escort you back to your rooms, dear ladies," Nicholas said as Aunt Rowena rose from the table. Gigi supported her until Nicholas reached her other side. With a flourish, he offered his arm to Aunt Rowena, then led her slowly out of the dining car.

Gigi took a moment to pack up the cards. When she finished, Professor Haskins was waiting for her.

As their gazes connected, he offered a soft smile. "Are you all right?"

"Me?"

"You seemed upset when Nicholas spoke back there."

Looking into the professor's hazel eyes, she wondered what he'd felt during the story. "I felt sorry for Nicholas, I guess," she said. "I wish he could find the happiness he seeks. I suppose his perspective now is much clearer than it was when he was younger."

"Something to think about, it seems." Professor Haskins extended his arm, and Gigi took it.

He walked slowly, and Gigi was grateful for it. She felt reluctant to be parted from him tonight. She'd grown comfortable around him, had become used to him, and looked forward to his every appearance, their every conversation. It was like he was a beloved brother . . . no, not a brother. A cousin? That was it. A male cousin she was very close to. No . . .

As they entered the corridor, the conductor at the other end of the train car turned his attention to the nearby window.

"There's that worry line again," Professor Haskins said, slowing.

"I have a worry line?"

With his other hand, he tapped the space between her brows. His touch was so light it could have been the wing of a butterfly. "Right there. Although it's so faint I doubt many would notice it."

He'd only touched her briefly, but she could still feel the warm brush of his finger.

"I didn't know I had a worry line," she said. "Perhaps I should frown more in the mirror, and then I could spot all the nefarious lines on my face."

He smiled and shook his head. "I wish you didn't have to worry or frown at all," he said, leading her now along the corridor. Casually, as if he hadn't just sent her heart racing.

"I blame it on Nicholas," Gigi said. "I wish I could bring something joyful to the man's life. Too bad Aunt Rowena is so much older than he."

The professor drew her to a stop at this, and typical of narrow corridors on a train, there was not much breathing space between them. Her arm was still linked in his, so when he turned slightly to look down at her, they were even closer.

"You are in earnest?" he asked. "Now who is the matchmaker, Miss Ballard?"

"I'm only teasing," she said, letting her smile escape. "I think Aunt Rowena would mow over any man brave enough to marry her."

The professor's chuckle was soft. "Perhaps you're right, but your aunt is not all that old."

"You're sweet," Gigi said. "She is sixty-five, and I'm guessing that Nicholas is but fifty."

"Sixty-five? I never would have guessed," Professor Haskins said, his eyes dancing. "The Ballard women must age well."

"Ah, be careful what you say," Gigi said. "Now I'm going to make you guess my age."

Professor Haskins didn't hesitate. "Twenty-one."

"No. I hope you're kidding." Gigi wanted to laugh, but she didn't want the others in their compartments to overhear.

"Twenty-four, then." The professor seemed to be standing closer to her now without moving an inch.

Or had the corridor somehow narrowed without her realizing it?

"That's quite a jump, and you're correct." At his smirk, she added, "You knew. How?"

"Your aunt might have mentioned it."

She smiled, and he smiled back. Time seemed to hover around them, not moving forward or backward.

The slide of a door somewhere along the corridor brought Gigi sharply into the present. "I should join my aunt and check if she needs assistance."

The professor nodded. "I'll see you in Vienna."

"Yes, until Vienna." She released his arm and walked the few paces to her compartment door. She paused before going in and glanced to where the professor still stood in the corridor.

He nodded at her, his mouth curved into a half smile.

She nodded back, then disappeared inside.

Aunt Rowena was sitting up in her bed, changed into her nightdress, her covers drawn about her. Without the glamour of her evening dress and pearls, she looked nearly a different person. Her eyes were wide as Gigi locked the compartment door.

"Do you think Nicholas has intentions on me?" Aunt Rowena asked in a hushed tone. "He was very conciliatory tonight, and I can't help but think he told us his sad tale of lost love in order to make me feel sympathetic."

Gigi blinked, trying to hold back a laugh. She supposed that some men younger than Aunt Rowena wouldn't be opposed to marrying an older woman . . . but fifteen years older?

"Professor Haskins knows him better than I do." Gigi slipped off her wrap and hung it up in the narrow closet. "Perhaps we can ask him in the morning. But I don't think the professor would have befriended him if the man is an opportunist." She winced the moment she said the word. She didn't want her aunt to think Gigi meant a younger man would only be interested in her aunt for her money.

"I don't think he's nefarious," her aunt mused, her gaze growing distant with thought. "I could see that he was being sincere, but I cannot take on a second spouse. Being married once was enough for me." She seemed to realize who her audience was and amended, "Not that marriage wasn't a wonderful experience. I am past my prime, and it's time to take care of me and not someone else."

"Yes, of course." Gigi moved in front of the small mirror and unpinned her hair. She ran a brush through the dull brown of her locks. Her thoughts turned to the Vittoria Caldoni painting and what Professor Haskins had said about her resemblance. Perhaps her brown hair wasn't so dull after all. The comparison had felt like a compliment at the time. Had it been? It was flattering—having a man compare her to a famous painting. But then again, he was an art history professor, and he likely equated many things in his life to art.

"Georgina," her aunt's voice cut into Gigi's thoughts. "What are you woolgathering about?"

Gigi looked at her aunt. What had the woman been saying? "I'm sorry. I suppose I'm tired."

"Of course, of course," Aunt Rowena said, her eyes taking on a speculative quality.

Gigi finished unpinning her hair, then changed into her nightdress. She turned down the gas lamp and slipped into bed between the pristine white sheets.

"Good night, Aunt," Gigi murmured, hoping sleep would soon overtake her circling thoughts.

"You are becoming quite close to the professor," Aunt Rowena said from the other side of the dark compartment.

Gigi drew in a breath. She had to be careful in her response. "We are merely friends. I think once he knew I was not pursuing him and that you were finished with your list, he has been able to be himself. I do not want to take that away from him."

Aunt Rowena remained silent for a moment. "Of course not, my dear."

There was more. Gigi could practically hear her aunt's mind turning.

"What if after all of this he falls in love with you?" Aunt Rowena said, her tone hopeful and nearly reverent. "He was affected by Nicholas's story tonight. I know it. A woman would have to be blind not to see that it gave him plenty to think about."

"That might be so," Gigi said. "But no one is going to matchmake on this trip. No one. I'd rather be friends with Professor Haskins than have him feel like I'm pursuing him."

"You're right," Aunt Rowena amended. "Of course you're right."

Gigi guessed if the gas lamp had still been on, she would have seen her aunt's eyes fill with anticipation.

"It's just so hard," Aunt Rowena said.

"What's so hard?" Gigi was truly curious now.

"Oh, you know . . . being with two perfectly compatible people who would be excellent in a marriage . . . and not being able to say one thing about it."

Gigi wanted to laugh. Her aunt had never kept her opinions silent. Perhaps Gigi could throw her off the professor's trail. "Do you remember Robert Pattens?"

Her aunt didn't answer at first. "The dark-haired man whose family owns the flower shop?"

"Yes, that's him," Gigi said. "When Lillian was in his shop the other day, he asked about the family and about *me* in particular." She hadn't thought too much about it at the time. Robert Pattens was a widower with two young children. If Gigi were to marry someone like him, she'd become an instant mother. A lot to consider.

"Did he?" Aunt Rowena's voice went up a notch. "His flower shop is quite successful, is it not?"

Gigi smiled in the darkness. "I believe so."

CHAPTER ELEVEN

Dear Lillian,

> *Vienna is beautiful. I don't even know how to describe it. The flowers, the shops, the food . . . yes, even the food is beautiful. This trip couldn't be going any better, and Aunt Rowena's ankle is fast healing. She's being pampered by her two friends, me, and of course, Professor Haskins. I've been impressed with his bedside manner, if you will. He insists that she is made comfortable everywhere we go.*
>
> *I can only write for a moment since Irene and I are going with the professor on a guided evening stroll. I'm so glad we're spending two full days in this city . . .*

THE TAP ON HER HOTEL room door brought Gigi fully into the present. She set down her sketchbook, where she'd been penciling a hat with waterproof material added to it. The thing was turning out to be ridiculous though.

"Irene must be here," Aunt Rowena called out from her bedroom in the two-room suite, where Blanche was visiting with her.

It turned out that Blanche didn't care for a guided evening stroll. Yet, Gigi would have loved to go with just Professor Haskins—not for romance or anything like that but because she loved every moment in his company. Their easy conversations. The way she felt alive and energetic around him. With Irene with them, surely the conversation would be much more proper.

"Ready?" Irene said as soon as Gigi opened the door. She wore a fur pelisse, and it reminded Gigi that she should bring something warmer. She chose a heavy shawl, then left the hotel room with Irene.

"I've always wanted to stroll in Vienna at sunset," Irene said as they headed for the lobby. "You're fortunate to have these experiences so young."

"I do feel fortunate," Gigi said. "I'm lucky my aunt invited me. This is certainly an experience I'll never forget."

Irene nodded. "I must say, I'm surprised that Rowena felt up to putting this trip together for all of us. What with her multiple doctor appointments." She stopped with a gasp, turning her wide eyes to Gigi.

"What are you talking about?" Gigi asked in a slow voice. "Is something the matter with my aunt?"

Irene closed her eyes, then released a slow breath.

Now Gigi was on full alert. "Please," she said, grasping Irene's arm. "What is it? Please tell me."

Irene looked down at her twisting hands. "I shouldn't have said a thing."

"I won't tell my aunt if that's what you're worried about—"

"Are you ladies ready?" a voice interrupted.

A voice Gigi was always glad to hear, but the timing couldn't have been worse. She turned and smiled at the approaching Professor Haskins. Even though Gigi's mind was trying to figure out what Irene had meant, her heart reacted to the sight of the professor. *Tap tap tap.*

He grasped Irene's hand with both of his and shook, then he turned to Gigi and did the same thing. She was tempted to cling to him, to tell him that her aunt was keeping a secret, and ask if he could help her.

But no. She only said, "We're ready."

"Wonderful." His smile was broad and cheerful, and he insisted that they each take one of his arms.

They headed out of the hotel and stepped onto the street into the setting sun. Orange and gold splashed across the buildings and a nearby bridge stretching across a narrow stream. The stream looked to be filled with glowing stars as the lively ripples caught that last light of day.

They didn't have to walk far before the professor located their walking guide. "There's our host, Mr. Becker."

"*Guten Abend*," Irene called out with a wave. She'd been spending the day learning German phrases.

The dark-haired man with a precise mustache grinned and waved back. "*Guten Abend*. Two beautiful ladies. My stars are lucky tonight."

Gigi smiled, but a weight had settled on her shoulders. She wanted to draw Irene aside and demand information. She couldn't think of any symptoms that Aunt Rowena had shown that might indicate a serious illness. For it would have to be serious if doctors were involved, right?

But their tour guide, Mr. Becker, was already beginning his narrative. Irene walked beside him while Professor Haskins and Gigi fell into step behind the pair. Not surprisingly, the professor offered his arm to Gigi.

"Thank you," she said with a smile, taking his arm.

But he wasn't fooled.

"What's the matter?" he asked in a low voice as Mr. Becker continued speaking in a loud enough voice for the three of them to hear.

She bit her lip and hesitated. Irene seemed completely focused on Mr. Becker and trying out more of her German.

"I can't . . ."

"Perhaps we can speak later?" Professor Haskins suggested.

Gigi nodded. She didn't know what she could tell him, except her worries. She tried to focus on Mr. Becker's words as he pointed out various locations. But soon she noticed she'd tightened her grip on the professor's arm. Had he noticed?

He said nothing, and she felt grateful for the companionship even though she couldn't tell him anything specific.

"Here we have a wonderful section of bakeries and chocolatiers," Mr. Becker continued. "Everything is made fresh on a daily basis."

"Is there anything I can do?" the professor asked in a low tone close to her ear.

"I don't know," Gigi whispered, glancing up, finding compassion in his hazel eyes. "Irene said something about my aunt being ill just before you came into the lobby. She acted as if she wasn't supposed to tell me. So, of course, now I'm very worried."

The professor's brows drew together. "I'm very sorry to hear it . . . whatever it is."

Gigi's throat burned with emotion, and she could only nod. She looked away from the professor's concerned eyes and tried to focus on the beauty of Vienna as they strolled along the walkway.

Then she felt a warm hand atop hers. She didn't pull away, didn't look over, but she knew the professor was trying to offer her comfort. This was not a romantic gesture. It was a friend helping another friend.

Her heart fully in her throat now, she glanced at him again. He was looking ahead, his expression seemingly lost in thought. But there was his hand, covering hers.

Irene hadn't noticed since her attention was still on Mr. Becker, and she hadn't looked back once.

Professor Haskins's hand was warm, comforting, reassuring, and although the knot of worry over her aunt still remained, she didn't feel alone in her worry.

The cool night air was fragrant as they reached a street with vibrant cafés. Light spilled from the doorways and windows. Music came and went. Sometimes faint, sometimes closer. And still the professor kept his hand over hers.

"Don't you think so?" Irene's voice floated back to them.

"What's that?" Professor Haskins asked.

Apparently he hadn't been paying attention to Irene and Mr. Becker's conversation either.

"Don't you think Vienna is the most romantic city?" Irene said, turning her smile upon them.

The professor slipped his hand away from Gigi's. "I believe it is," he rumbled.

Gigi understood why he'd moved his hand, but she wished he hadn't. It was for the best though. If Irene saw them hold hands, she'd take the news straight to Aunt Rowena.

"It is beautiful," Gigi added, hoping the emotion in her voice didn't show through. Worry about her aunt, combined with the sweet gesture of the professor, was making her heart soar and dip alternately.

"If only I were thirty years younger and I had my Benedict with me," Irene said, her tone wistful. "We spent all our years raising children and never taking time for ourselves. By the time our youngest had up and married, Benedict's health had declined too greatly. We never got to fulfill our dreams."

Gigi glanced at the professor at the same time he looked at her. Their gazes met, and Gigi wished she could know what was going through his mind right now.

"You are still young, madame," Mr. Becker said in stilted English. "And you have many years of beauty left."

Irene laughed. "You are a kind man, sir."

He said something in German that sounded like an endearment, and Irene laughed again.

"Our Mr. Becker seems quite besotted with Irene," the professor whispered.

"What is he saying to her?"

"*Eine Frau wird erst mit zunehmendem Alter schöner.* A woman only grows more beautiful with age."

Gigi smiled. "That is nice. German sounds more romantic than I expected."

The professor nodded. "I suppose. Of course, a place like this makes it easy."

He was right. The velvety darkness, the quiet stream, the glowing lights, the soft music, the man beside her . . .

She exhaled. She was bewitched. Soon they'd return to the hotel and reality would set in as she asked her aunt about her health.

Gigi soaked in the sights and listened to the sounds of the evening around her. She tried to understand why her aunt hadn't told her of her illness, and she tried to make sense of the feelings battling inside her about the man walking with her. He'd become a friend, a confidante, and beyond that . . . no, she couldn't presume anything.

"When we get back to the hotel, do you want me to come with you to speak to your aunt?"

She met the professor's gaze. Darkness had fallen, and lights glittered all around, but his eyes were as dark as the night. The offer was so kind, and she wished that their relationship wouldn't be at an end when this tour was over.

"I must do this alone," she said. "But thank you for your offer. She might not be too happy that I've found out."

The professor nodded, then he reached for her hand again. This time, he drew it toward him and pressed a kiss on her knuckles. He didn't release her right away, and charging horses couldn't have enticed her to pull her hand away from his touch.

"Send word if you change your mind," he said.

"I will. Thank you." Her voice was only a whisper because her throat had tightened. She would miss this man. Dearly.

They'd neared their hotel again, and the four of them paused outside the entrance. Mr. Becker was dishing out the compliments to Irene, and she was laughing and blushing—something Gigi might have laughed over herself if she hadn't been worried about her aunt.

After bidding farewell to Mr. Becker, the three of them walked into the hotel and paused in the lobby.

"It has been a lovely evening, ladies," the professor said, shaking both of their hands once again.

Gigi thought Professor Haskins might have lingered over shaking her hand, and his gaze held hers for a moment longer—seeming to say that he wanted her to send for him if needed.

As she and Irene headed out of the lobby, Gigi didn't waste a moment. "You must tell me about my aunt's condition."

"It's not for me to tell," Irene said, the smiles of the night gone now. "I shouldn't have said anything."

"I'm glad you did." Gigi linked her arm with Irene's. "Is it awful? My imagination has been spinning all night."

Regret crossed Irene's face. "I am sorry for that. I do apologize."

"Don't you see?" Gigi said. "I don't care about a ruined night. I'm worried about my aunt."

Irene squeezed her hand. "Let me confess to Rowena first, and then she can tell you."

So when they arrived at Gigi's hotel room, Irene went inside first, and Gigi stayed in the sitting area. From the murmured voices that she couldn't quite distinguish, it sounded like Irene was getting a set down. Moments later, both Irene and Blanche came out, their faces drawn and pale.

"I'm sorry," Irene said once again.

Blanche only offered a grim nod, then both of the women were gone, leaving Gigi in the hotel room with only Aunt Rowena.

She walked toward her aunt's bedroom, both determined and reluctant.

Aunt Rowena sat propped in bed, already wearing her nightdress. She held her favorite book of poems in her lap as if she'd been reading when Irene had arrived. Or perhaps she'd been reading aloud to Blanche.

"Aunt—" Gigi began.

"Sit down, dear," Aunt Rowena said.

Gigi obeyed and sat in the wingback chair across from the bed. She clasped her hands together tightly, her stomach churning in knots.

"I have a mass in my upper stomach," Aunt Rowena said without preamble. "The doctor won't know if it's cancerous until they perform surgery to remove it."

Gigi stared at her aunt. Cancer? Surgery? She couldn't process all of this at once. "When? How? And why . . . why are we here? You need surgery."

Aunt Rowena raised a hand. "Listen to me, dear. The mass has been there for probably months. What's another month? Yes, the doctor recommended immediate surgery, but if it's cancer . . . then there is the possibility it has already spread throughout my body."

Gigi covered her mouth, holding back a gasp. Aunt Rowena had been living with this knowledge this entire trip? How . . . ?

"Because of that risk, I knew that once I had the surgery, my life would change." She smoothed back a part of her hair with a trembling hand. "I might never get a chance to travel again."

The depth of Aunt Rowena's blue eyes told Gigi what her aunt feared the most.

"Are the doctors saying . . . ?" She couldn't finish. Aunt Rowena held out her hand, and Gigi rushed over to grasp it. "I don't want to lose you."

"Whatever happens," Aunt Rowena said in a steady voice, "we will enjoy this trip and make the best memories we can."

CHAPTER TWELVE

Dear Lillian,

> *Last night I went on a romantic evening stroll through Vienna. No, I wasn't kissed or proposed to, but romance doesn't always need to be with one's true love. Vienna is beautiful and romantic. Irene Martin and Professor Haskins were with me, along with our tour guide, the charming Mr. Becker. You should have heard Irene practicing her German. It all sounded Greek to me. And the professor speaks fair German too . . .*

GIGI DECIDED NOT TO TELL Lillian about Aunt Rowena's illness. The thought of her aunt in need of urgent surgery made her feel sick. What if . . . what if they were wasting precious time and the delay in surgery would be followed by a more serious outcome?

Gigi concluded her letter, then left the hotel room to post it with the concierge. It was still early in the morning, and Aunt Rowena wouldn't rise for at least two more hours. But Gigi had slept fitfully at best. She walked through the nearly silent hotel and handed the letter over to the concierge.

Outside, the sun was just rising, the pale yellow of the breaking dawn softening the deeper violet sky. Gigi walked outside and headed toward the nearby bridge that led across a quaint stream. It was too early for shoppers to be out, but there were a few people about, opening bakeries and such.

Gigi walked to the center of the bridge and rested her hands on the cool stone of the railing. The peaceful stream below should have brought her some calmness, but her thoughts and mind were still racing. Her aunt was one stubborn woman. Gigi wondered what her mother and sister would think when they found out. Life was too precious to go against a doctor's orders. Before long, Gigi's eyes were burning with threatening tears.

Despite all of her aunt's faux pas, Gigi didn't want harm to come to the woman, and she hated to think that she'd been suffering for any amount of time. If only her father were alive, he'd know what to do. His decisive personality was sorely needed right now. Gigi closed her eyes as the cool breeze lifted from the water.

Could she continue the rest of the tour without turning every moment into frustrating worry that was out of her control? Could she put faith in her aunt's decision? Could Gigi be cheerful and focus on the here and now and not dwell upon what the future might bring?

"I don't know," she whispered to herself.

"Miss Ballard?"

She startled and turned, opening her eyes. At the base of the bridge, Professor Haskins was gazing up at her. He wore no hat or jacket, only his shirtsleeves, as if he hadn't quite prepared himself for the day.

"I saw you from my hotel room window," he said, walking up the bridge to stand before her. "I was worried . . ."

His voice trailed off because she hadn't been able to hide her tears.

"Are you all right?"

She wanted to say, *Yes, I'm all right*, but that's not what came out of her mouth. "It's all worse than I feared. I don't know what to do." Then it seemed as if a great tidal wave of emotion crashed into her, and her breath hitched as a sob escaped. "I–I'm sorry." She turned from him, burying her face in her hands because she wasn't about to cry in front of him.

He had every right to express his condolences, then leave her to her tears.

But he didn't leave. He pulled her into his arms, right there on the bridge. They didn't know anyone in Vienna, but Gigi hesitated nonetheless. Then she gave in. She no longer cared about propriety or what her acquaintances might say. She wrapped her arms about Professor Haskins and buried her face against his shirt. The cotton fabric was thin enough that she could feel the warmth of his chest through it and smell the soap on his skin.

His hands moved up her back, and he whispered, "Can you tell me, or is it a great secret?"

She almost smiled despite her tears. "It's a great secret."

"Ah."

His arms seemed to fit about her perfectly, and his chest seemed to be crafted as the best place to lay her head. These thoughts should not be intruding at a time like this. Professor Haskins was her friend. She cared about him, and he cared about her . . . as friends. This was a rare jewel among relationships, and she didn't want him to think she was acting on theatrics to get him to hold her in his arms.

So she straightened her spine and drew away from him. With steely resolve, she wiped at her cheeks and swallowed back the lump in her throat. "I am sorry about my outburst. I didn't sleep well last night, and I'm overly tired. I have got to get a better handle on this before I return to my aunt this morning."

Professor Haskins grasped both of her hands. "Miss Ballard, don't apologize. You're upset. You don't have to confess anything to me, but know that I'd love to help in any way that I can. Whatever it might be."

The sincerity in his tone nearly brought on another round of tears. But she bit her lip, holding them at bay. She breathed in, then out, then in. Lifting her chin, she met the professor's gaze. In the changing light of dawn, his hazel eyes were more green than brown. His warm hands enfolded her cold ones, and she wanted to never let go.

"I don't know if I can tell you," she said in a halting tone. "She didn't even tell me and wouldn't have on this trip if it weren't for Irene."

The professor lightly squeezed her hands. "What if I guess?"

She hesitated, then said, "All right."

So he guessed and guessed until he hit upon the word *cancer*, and she nodded.

He paused, his brows pulled together. "Truly?"

"Suspected," she said. "They can't know for sure until . . ."

"Until she has surgery?" he finished for her.

"Correct." She bit her lip again, but this time, it wasn't enough to stop the tears.

Professor Haskins produced a handkerchief. She hadn't yet returned the last one he'd given her. Slowly, carefully, he pressed the soft cloth against her cheeks.

She closed her eyes as he administered to her. The world around them had lightened enough that anyone who knew them could easily recognize them. But still, she didn't move, didn't pull away, and instead soaked in his strong, steady presence and was grateful she had such a friend—one who could bring her companionship and comfort at a time like this.

"Can I assume that your aunt did not follow her doctor's orders but instead booked this trip?"

Gigi's eyes fluttered open. "She didn't want me to miss out on the opportunity of meeting you, and she said that after the surgery she might never travel again."

"Ah." The professor tucked the handkerchief into her hand. "She is certainly a woman of determination."

Gigi smiled, but she felt like crying at the same moment. "Determination is a gentle way of saying how stubborn she is."

Professor Haskins returned her smile. "Yes, but you love her anyway."

Her voice fell a notch. "Yes. She has been a glue to our family ever since our father—her brother—passed away. I don't know how my mother would have pulled through without Aunt Rowena."

The air was warming quickly, and the morning had brightened. But the professor didn't step back, didn't release the hand he was still holding. In fact, he leaned closer and spoke quietly. "I am at your service, Miss Ballard."

Only then did he release her hand and step away.

"Thank you," she whispered, gazing into his hazel eyes that had lightened and taken on some gold with the rising sun. Looking at him standing in front of the backdrop of Vienna was like looking at a painting, but even a renowned painter couldn't have captured what her eyes were seeing. For the first time, she understood the struggle an artist had of trying to convey both form and emotion in an image on canvas.

"I'll have a meal sent to your room so that you can rest," the professor said.

Gigi hesitated. Her exhaustion was catching up to her, but she didn't want to be a burden on anyone.

"Georgina," the professor said softly. "I insist that you rest."

She gazed at him across the few feet that separated them. The breeze had ruffled his hair, and he hadn't shaved yet this morning. His eyes were kind, compassionate, and warm. She could easily get lost in those eyes if she stood here much longer.

"All right," she said. "But I'll be up for our tour this afternoon."

His mouth curved. "Very well."

She walked past him then, although he joined her side by the time she reached the bottom of the bridge. They said nothing as they walked the short distance to the hotel. When Professor Haskins reached for the hotel door to open it, Gigi said, "You can call me Gigi."

His gaze shifted to hers, and she saw both surprise and warmth there.

"My aunt is the only one who calls me Georgina," she continued, "because I am named after her. Rowena Georgina Ballard II."

"The second?"

"Yes, the second. All very formal, you know."

"Duly noted." The professor smiled, and it was as if all the heat of the sun hit her at that exact moment. "Gigi it is. After you, my friend."

She stepped past him into the hotel lobby. *My friend.* They were sweet words, to be sure. Words she hoped to always deserve.

Once inside her hotel room, Gigi found her aunt in the sitting area. She was still in her nightdress, but she had her notebook with her and was writing in it.

"You're awake early," Gigi said, crossing to her aunt.

Aunt Rowena looked up and gave her a faint smile, not her usual cheerful one. And her skin seemed pale, although she'd dabbed some rouge on her cheekbones.

"Are you all right?" Gigi sat on the settee closest to her aunt's chair.

"I'm fine, dear," Aunt Rowena said. "I'm planning out the next two days. I want to make sure the professor doesn't miss anything at the Belvedere Museum today."

Gigi told herself to relax. Her aunt might look a bit pale, but she was talking like nothing was amiss. "I'm sure he's well prepared."

Aunt Rowena nodded, looked down at her notebook, then peered up at Gigi again. "Where have you been so early, Georgina?"

"I posted a letter to Lillian."

Aunt Rowena's brows lifted.

"And I spoke to the professor," she said. "Apparently, he was an early bird too this morning."

At this, Aunt Rowena gave a genuine smile, and some color returned to her face. "How lovely. You are becoming such good friends. Do you think there will ever be a possibility—"

"No." Gigi raised her hand. "We are friends, that is all." She should be annoyed—her aunt wasn't letting this drop—but she felt no annoyance. How could she? There were more important things to worry about.

"Well, I, for one, wouldn't be opposed to a match between the two of you."

"I think you've made that clear."

Aunt Rowena chuckled. "I believe you're right." She sobered and said, "Now, tell me what's troubling you. You look like you haven't slept."

Gigi looked down at her clasped hands. "Professor Haskins knows you're sick. He guessed and now . . ." She looked up at her aunt.

"Now he wants to send me home to the doctor?"

"No," Gigi rushed to say. "Nothing like that. He only offered his services. Whatever we need."

Aunt Rowena gave a thoughtful nod. "He's a good man through and through. But my decision still stands. And my wish right now is that we move on from this conversation. I already made this decision, and it's not up for debate."

Gigi nodded.

"Now, off with you," Aunt Rowena said. "Even a blind bat could see that you need sleep."

Gigi rose to her feet and kissed her aunt's cheek, then walked to her bedroom on the other side of the suite. As she climbed into the bed and pulled the covers over her, the exhaustion seemed to multiply all at once. She was grateful that her aunt hadn't been too upset that Professor Haskins knew about her condition.

Her last thought before she drifted off to sleep was how nice it was when Professor Haskins had hugged her. She'd felt truly comforted. And she hoped that nothing would ever happen to change their friendship.

CHAPTER THIRTEEN

Dear Lillian,

Our final day in Vienna was more than perfect. We leave in just a few hours on the Orient Express for Bucharest. I can hardly believe that I am now a world traveler. Using the names of these cities in conversation and knowing that I've been there is a heady feeling. Aunt Rowena's ankle is on the mend, and she is excellent at ordering everyone around—not that she ever had trouble in the first place.

I know that I've mentioned Professor Haskins in nearly all of my letters, but I just learned that he knows three other languages fluently. I'm astounded. Can you guess which ones? Since you're not in the same room as me, I'll tell you: English. Fooling there—that one doesn't count, right? French, German, and . . . Hungarian. I would have never guessed Hungarian in a hundred years. But apparently, his great-grandmother is from Hungary, so he took it upon himself to learn the language. Even though he's never met her . . .

"ANYONE NEED ANYTHING FROM ANY of the shops?" the professor asked as the tour group lounged in the lobby. Their luggage was already on the way to the train station, and everyone was either visiting the shops or relaxing in the hotel lobby before their transportation arrived.

"I've outwalked myself today," Irene said, draping her arm over her brow.

Professor Haskins smiled. "All right then. Mrs. Martin is out. Anyone else interested?"

Aunt Rowena had been a trooper all day, but now she was keeping her foot propped on a stool while she sat in a plush lounge chair.

"Blanche and Georgina should go," Irene said with a sigh. "Fetch me some of the divine Austrian chocolate."

Gigi wanted to laugh, and she saw the amusement in the professor's eyes too.

"If I go into one more shop, I'll be broke," Blanche said with a smile so everyone knew she was teasing. "Rowena and Georgina should go."

"I'm perfectly comfortable," Aunt Rowena stated. "Georgina, you should go pick out something for yourself. You've only bought gifts for your sister and mother. Besides, the professor can't go alone."

Gigi didn't answer, didn't move. Was her aunt really endorsing, or encouraging, her to go alone with the professor? Of course, they wouldn't technically be alone. People were in every shop and all over the streets. She could feel the professor's gaze upon her, watching, waiting for her decision.

She rose to her feet. "Well, I suppose I shouldn't let a walk through Vienna go to waste. How many times can I say that in my life?"

Aunt Rowena chuckled. "Not many, dear. Enjoy yourselves, and we'll see you soon. We can't miss the train, mind you."

"Never." Gigi bade farewell to the other women, then walked with the professor out of the hotel. The afternoon had advanced enough that the heat had simmered down, and the cooling breeze stirred the bottom of her skirt.

Without a word, the professor offered his arm, and Gigi rested her hand in the crook of his elbow. This casual walking with him was becoming so familiar to her.

Their first stop was a toymaker shop. "We're going in here?" Gigi asked.

"We sure are." Professor Haskins opened the door for her.

Gigi stepped inside what she could only describe as a fairy-tale world. Toys, dolls, puppets, board games, and sweets filled every nook and cranny of the store. A hooting sound came from above, and she looked up to see a miniature train on a miniature track chugging near the ceiling.

She turned in a slow circle, feeling like she was a small child in a candy shop who was just told she could buy something.

"This is amazing," she said as she faced the professor again.

He grinned. "I'm glad you think so. Every time I come to Vienna, I visit this shop and add to my collection."

"What are you collecting?"

"Come and see." The professor moved deeper into the shop, where a tiny woman stood behind a cash register, apparently absorbed in a thick book. She glanced up at them, nodded once, then returned to her book.

"Look," Professor Haskins said, drawing Gigi to a stop. He picked up a small train car that was similar to the running train above them. The car he held in his hands was painted bright blue and had sticks inside to represent tiny logs.

"You're building your own train?" Gigi said, marveling at the exacting detail of the train car.

"I am," he said. "I have eight cars now, and this will be number nine."

"I love them," she said, and she did. Their miniature perfection was enchanting. "How do you limit yourself to only buying one at a time? I'd want the whole train set at once."

"That takes the fun out of collecting," he said in a lowered tone, as if he didn't want the shopkeeper to overhear. "In fact, I don't think it would be considered collecting at all. More like . . ."

"Buying?"

"Correct."

She loved his smile, his wit, his caring concern, his thoughtfulness . . . and how he bought a single train car each time he was in Vienna.

"You should start collecting something," he said. "From this very shop. You have a wide array of choices."

"But they're all toys . . ." She winced. "I didn't mean—"

"I know what you meant," he said, his smile soft. "Look around. See what you think. I don't think the *fräulein* would mind."

Gigi stifled a laugh. "Maybe I will." She moved among the displays, picking up a few things, considering. Her eyes were continuously drawn to a set of teacups. Children's teacups, to be sure, but they were delicately painted and simply irresistible. Lillian would laugh at Gigi if she showed up at home with this purchase.

"Buy it," Professor Haskins whispered next to her ear.

She flinched at his unexpected nearness; she'd been so lost in her own thoughts. When she turned to face him, he didn't give her very much space. Not that she minded. Well, she should mind, but she didn't. "I never had a teacup set as a little girl," she said with a shrug. "Maybe it would, oh, I don't know, make me feel . . ." She had no idea what she was saying.

"Happy?" The professor picked up one of the teacups. The rosebud painted on the side was surrounded by pale green leaves. "If a child's teacup brings you happiness, then I think you must have it." His gaze shifted to hers. "I'll buy it for you."

"Oh, no," she said. "I couldn't let you do that. I'll buy it."

He hesitated, then said, "All right. Let's go ring up our purchases so we don't run out of time."

There were still two hours at least before they had to return to the hotel. "Why would we run out of time? What are you planning, Professor?"

"Clyde," he said in a whisper. "When it's just us, call me Clyde."

Gigi glanced at the shopkeeper, then met the professor's gaze again. "All right, Clyde. What are you planning?"

He grinned. "You'll have to wait and see."

She wanted to slug his arm, but he moved past her too quickly. Soon they'd both bought their collector's items, and the professor—Clyde—tucked the bundle under one arm, then offered her his other arm.

"I can't believe I'm an official collector," she said. "It feels exhilarating."

She felt his smile before she heard his laugh—a laugh she was beginning to count on, to rely on, and to look forward to.

As they walked along the cobblestone road, Gigi absorbed the peace of their surroundings, studied the shops and homes, and observed the people they passed.

"I could live here," she announced.

Clyde looked at her with a half smile. "Is that so?"

"I mean, I'd have to learn German, of course," she said. "But I'm sure living in Vienna would only help me learn it faster."

"You have a point there," he said in a conciliatory tone. "And I could visit you each time I'm in Vienna, a sort of a reunion between friends."

Friends . . . There was that word again. "Of course. You could stop by my home and view my growing collection of children's teacups."

"Ah, so you are already picking out your home, are you?"

"Why yes," she said, stifling a laugh. "It will be on this road."

Professor Haskins slowed his step, which meant she slowed as well. He was grinning now. "Which house are you speaking of? Just so I know where to come visit you and your, uh, teacups."

She pointed across the street to a charming blue-and-yellow home nestled tight between two other homes. "It will likely be that one. I just have to convince the owner to sell it to me."

The professor chuckled. "I'm sure you'll have no trouble. Let's hope he, or she, speaks some English."

Gigi wrinkled her nose. "Let's hope."

They continued to walk, and soon, the professor drew her to a stop again. "This is our second stop," he said, guiding her to a bakery.

At least it looked like a bakery from the outside, but inside, it was . . . heaven.

"Chocolate," Gigi breathed. And that was an understatement. The shop was a chocolatier, and an exquisite one at that. A long glass counter stretched across one side of the shop and tiny lights illuminated the delectable creations.

"Heavens," Gigi murmured as she peered into the case, with its rows of chocolate perfection. "Does it taste as good as it looks?"

"Better." The professor nodded to the shopkeeper, a long, skinny fellow with an impressive mustache.

The shopkeeper slid open one side of the case and held his glinting silver tongs over the array of choices.

The professor pointed to one of the trays, and the shopkeeper removed a dark-chocolate truffle with a pink-laced frosting design.

When he set it in front of Gigi, the shopkeeper produced a small silver knife. Slowly, he cut the truffle in two, then stood back.

"Try it," the professor said.

"It's too pretty to eat," Gigi said, but her hand had a mind of its own. Before she knew it, she'd picked up one half of the truffle and popped it into her mouth.

Professor Haskins smiled, picked up the other half, and put the piece into his mouth.

Their gazes connected, then Gigi's eyes slid shut. Chocolate this rich and creamy deserved every bit of her focus. She couldn't look at anything or allow for any distraction. It was just her and the taste buds on her tongue wondering how one might live in Vienna and visit this shop every single day for the rest of her life.

She savored the magnificent flavor, then finally, slowly opened her eyes.

The professor was watching her, a half smile on his face, his hazel eyes amused. "You show your feelings when you eat something you love."

"And I loved that truffle." She was blushing. From chocolate? Or because of the man who was so carefully and slowly becoming part of her heart?

Professor Haskins turned to the shopkeeper. "We'll take two dozen wrapped in two parts."

Before Gigi could speak, he lifted his hand as if to stop any argument. "Your aunt and her friends must try them. Don't you agree?"

"Yes, otherwise I would eat them all."

The professor smiled. "We still have others to try."

And they did. Gigi sampled other types of chocolate, and although it was all divine, nothing compared to the truffles. Once the shopkeeper rang up their order—which the professor paid for entirely—they headed out into the warm sunshine.

"This could possibly be the best day of my life," Gigi said.

Professor Haskins chuckled.

"Oh, did I say that aloud?"

"You did."

She linked arms with him as they began to stroll. "I think I'd better carry the sack with the chocolates to keep them safe."

The professor handed over the sack. "I wouldn't have it any other way."

CHAPTER
FOURTEEN

Dear Lillian,

Prepare yourself. Upon my arrival home, you will taste heaven itself. Professor Haskins and I found the best chocolatier shop. I'm bringing the truffles home for you to taste. I'll just have to find a way to keep them preserved—as in, to not eat them all beforehand.

We've left beautiful Vienna, and I plan on taking up German studies the moment I return home. I am determined to one day revisit Vienna. I have no idea when, but it is now my dream. I hope I'm not boring you with stories about the professor, but I discovered he is a collector—of toy trains. Imagine. And he's been quite influential apparently because I've decided to collect children's teacups. We found a charming toy shop . . .

GIGI WENT TO BED WITH a smile on her face, but hours later, she awoke with a start in the darkness of the train compartment. They were on their way to Bucharest. The sounds she heard were familiar: the motion of the train and the faint rumble that had become strangely soothing. So what had awakened her?

Then she heard a soft groan.

"Aunt Rowena?" Gigi sat up and pushed her covers aside. The only light came from the thin crack of the doorway. But it was hardly enough to see anything. She reached for the gas lamp on the table where she knew it was. Moments later, the compartment was bathed in soft light.

Aunt Rowena lay in bed, her back turned to Gigi. She'd kicked off her covers, and she looked like a small, huddled child.

Another moan sent Gigi scrambling across the room. She placed a hand on her aunt's shoulder. "What is it? Did you have a bad dream? Are you ill?"

Her aunt didn't speak but only moaned again.

Gigi's heart hammered, and she leaned over to place a hand on her aunt's forehead. Her skin felt like fire. "Do you want some water?" She turned to search for the glass of water that she filled each night for her aunt. Locating it, she sat next to her. "Here, try some water."

Aunt Rowena turned her head, and Gigi nearly recoiled at the sickly paleness of her aunt's face.

Gigi slipped one hand behind her aunt's neck and helped lift her head to take a sip of water. Only one sip.

"Can you drink more?" Gigi asked.

Aunt Rowena shook her head, then winced.

"What's wrong? Is it your stomach? Your head?"

"Everything," her aunt whispered. "I'm too hot, then too cold, and I feel like my limbs are made of stone. I can barely move."

"I will alert the conductor," Gigi said, setting the glass on the small table. "There has to be someone on board who can help. Perhaps a doctor."

Aunt Rowena looked as if she wanted to say something. Instead, her eyes slid shut, and she exhaled.

Please be well, Gigi thought as she pulled on a robe and tied it close. There was no time for dressing or doing up her hair. She slipped out of the compartment, her worry pushing against her throat. Looking left, she saw that the conductor's post was abandoned. Where had he gone? Surely he was nearby. She decided to head to the dining car. Perhaps someone else was awake. Otherwise, she'd need to enter another train car corridor to find the conductor. In the worst case, she'd have to begin knocking on compartment doors and rousing other passengers.

Gigi clutched her robe about her as she hurried along the corridor. She entered the dining car to find it empty, save for a lone man sitting at one of the tables, his attention focused on a newspaper. His all-black attire and smokeless pipe made her recognize him instantly.

Nicholas.

"Sir, can you help me?" she rushed to say.

His chin snapped up. He stared at her for a second, then stood abruptly. "Vhat is it, Miss Ballard?"

"It's my aunt. She's ill with a fever and looks frightfully pale." Gigi swallowed. "She's . . . she might have cancer, but I don't know if that's what's wrong right now or—"

"A doctor is on zeh train," Nicholas said, crossing to her. "I'll find out his compartment number from zeh conductor and bring him to your aunt right away."

Gigi wanted to sag with relief, to cry with happiness, but she had to get back to her aunt. "Thank you, sir. Thank you. I can't express how much—"

Nicholas rested a hand on her shoulder. "Return to your aunt. I'll bring zeh doctor as soon as I can."

Gigi nodded, feeling numb. Perhaps this was all a bad dream and she'd awaken in a few moments relieved. But no, Nicholas had already disappeared down the corridor, and her aunt was likely miserable with whatever affliction was plaguing her.

Soon, Gigi slipped into the shared compartment. Aunt Rowena was still in the same position. She hadn't moved. Her eyes were closed, and Gigi watched for a moment to determine that her aunt was still breathing.

Tears stinging her eyes, Gigi returned to her aunt's bedside and placed a hand on her forehead. Still hot. Next she clasped her aunt's hand. It, too, was overly warm and clammy.

"A doctor is coming, Aunt," Gigi said. "I found Nicholas in the dining car, and he said there's a doctor on the train."

Aunt Rowena exhaled. "Thank you," she whispered, then squeezed Gigi's hand.

Now all they had to do was wait. The minutes ticked by agonizingly slowly as Gigi wondered which train car the doctor was in.

When a soft knock sounded at the door, Gigi flinched. She crossed to the door and opened it. There stood a short, round man, appearing hastily dressed. Behind him stood Nicholas, tall and stoic.

"*Darf ich rein kommen?*"

"He wants permission to enter and examine your aunt," Nicholas said.

"Yes, yes, of course." Gigi stepped aside and motioned for the doctor to enter.

Nicholas remained in the corridor; there simply wasn't room for anyone else inside the compartment.

Gigi relocated everything on the table before the doctor set a medical bag atop it. As the doctor spoke German to Aunt Rowena, Nicholas softly translated. Gigi watched the examination and how her aunt seemed to rally a bit, knowing that she had a doctor's help.

When he began asking her questions about her health history, Gigi bit her lip at the translations Nicholas gave between the two of them. The doctor had plenty of questions about her pending surgery. The doctor's manner was brusque, and after a few more questions, he packed up his things and turned to Nicholas.

Gigi wished she could follow the German, but she had to wait for Nicholas's translation.

"She must mix zis powder in vith vater and drink it three times a day until she can meet vith her doctor at home," Nicholas translated.

The German doctor nodded, then said something else to Nicholas.

"And . . ." Nicholas hesitated and glanced at Aunt Rowena.

"What is it?" Gigi asked.

Nicholas glanced at the doctor, who gave a firm nod. "Zeh doctor wants her to return home immediately. He says zaht if she does have cancer, zehn it will lower her immune system. She might have a small illness now, but it vill be made vorse because of zeh condition of her health."

Gigi nodded, her mind racing with too many questions to respond. They were on a train to Bucharest. How did one reverse their route? She had enough clarity to thank the doctor before he left.

She leaned against the door after she closed it behind the men. How did she approach her aunt about this? Surely Aunt Rowena had overheard, even though her eyes were closed again.

Gigi crossed to her aunt's bed and sat beside her. "Tell me what you want to do," she whispered.

But her aunt didn't respond. It seemed that she'd fallen asleep.

The hours of the night passed slowly. Gigi didn't sleep at all as she listened for any change of breathing from her aunt. As the compartment lightened with the approaching dawn glinting between the velvet drapes, Gigi knew she had to speak to her aunt's friends. But first she roused her aunt to give her the powder mixed with water.

Aunt Rowena opened her eyes, and her usually bright blue eyes were now dull.

"How are you feeling?" Gigi asked, placing a hand on her forehead again. Her aunt's forehead was still warm but not as hot. That must be a good sign.

"I'm so tired," her aunt said. "I feel like I've been awake for days and days."

"The doctor left you more powder to put in some water," Gigi said. "Here, let me help you sit up." She helped her aunt move into a sitting position.

After she drank half of the mixture, Aunt Rowena leaned back on her pillow. "I will be fine," she said, closing her eyes once again with a sigh. "I'll just rest today in the hotel, and you can join the tour."

"You need to be watched over," Gigi said. How could her aunt say she would be fine? She couldn't even keep her eyes open, and a doctor had needed to be fetched in the middle of the night. Gigi hated that it had come to this, but she was left with no other choice.

"The doctor said we need to cut the trip short," Gigi said gently. "He says your immunity is lower because of the cancer inside your body."

Aunt Rowena's eyes opened at that. "We don't know if it's cancer." She pushed up on her elbows, but even that movement left her breathless. "They won't know until surgery, and I won't have a doctor who knows nothing about my condition order me around. Besides, I don't want my ball gowns to go to waste. The professor said that, on the way back, we'd detour to Salzburg and attend a ball with the Salzburg Maestro. He's the most revered musician and composer in all of Europe. I brought two ball gowns so that I could decide between them."

Gigi would have laughed if her aunt hadn't been so earnest. In fact, Gigi wondered if Aunt Rowena was a tad delirious. She certainly wasn't thinking straight. This was the first Gigi had heard of a ball with the Maestro, but it didn't matter; Gigi hadn't brought her ball gown anyway.

A knock sounded on the door, saving Gigi from responding. Perhaps someone else could help her convince her aunt that things like balls and ball gowns were not important right now. Gigi opened the door, expecting to see Irene or Blanche there, but it was Professor Haskins.

"I hope I didn't disturb you," he said in a low voice. "Nicholas told me about your aunt's illness."

Gigi glanced back at her aunt. "It's the professor. I'll be back in a moment." She stepped into the corridor and slid the door closed behind her so that her aunt would have her privacy while still in bed.

The professor's gaze was concerned as he studied her. Gigi had been fine, had been strong, until now. Emotions rushed through her, all of her fears about her aunt, all of her doubts about staying on the trip this long. "The doctor has advised us to return home as quickly as possible but . . ." Her throat tightened, and the words were lost.

"She does not want to go?" the professor guessed.

Gigi nodded.

"I don't want her to go either," he said. "But I spoke with the doctor after Nicholas told me. The doctor makes a good argument. Your aunt is putting her health at risk in more ways than one."

The words felt like a stone in her stomach. The doctor had said the same thing last night, and, hearing Professor Haskins repeat it now only made it all the more real.

"Gigi," he said in a soft voice, clasping her hand. "If I could come with you, I would. But—"

"You have other members on the tour. I know," she said, clinging to his hand. His grasp was solid and warm, and she needed his steadiness right now. "I understand, and I'd never expect you to come with us. It's not like you're . . . family."

His smile was faint, and he lifted his other hand to smooth back a bit of hair from her face. "Even so, I wish I could come."

The intensity of his gaze made her stomach do a full somersault. She would miss this man. If only her aunt weren't ill, then she'd have more time with him. But that was a selfish thought.

"Will you talk to her?" Gigi said, her voice trembling now. "I'm afraid I'm not able to get past her stubbornness, and she thinks so highly of you. She's upset about missing the ball with the Salzburg Maestro. I didn't know there would be a ball."

"Ah," the professor said with a sigh. "That type of thing is optional, and now I'm sorry she'll be disappointed." He fixed her with a look that Gigi wasn't sure she understood.

"What is it?"

"I don't typically go to them," he said. "I leave that to the guests. But I might have changed my mind to be there with you."

Gigi couldn't quite catch a full breath.

"Georgina," a voice said from the other side of the door.

Gigi pushed back the heat climbing up her throat. "Could you speak to her?"

"Of course."

"Wait here a moment." Gigi ducked back into the room to find Aunt Rowena trying to get out of bed. Her face was flushed with exertion, and perspiration stood out on her brow.

"Aunt, what are you doing?" Gigi asked, hurrying to her side. "You're to stay in bed at the very least."

Aunt Rowena settled back onto the bed, her breathing coming in gasps. "What did the professor want?"

"He's spoken with the doctor, and . . . the professor agrees. We should head home to get you better."

Aunt Rowena closed her eyes, saying nothing.

"He'd like to speak with you if that's all right."

She nodded and opened her eyes. "All right."

So Gigi opened the door for the professor and invited him inside.

"My dear madam," the professor said, crossing to her bed. "I'm so sorry you've been ill."

Aunt Rowena's eyes filled with tears, and the professor took her hand in his.

"We will book you on the very next tour once you've recovered from surgery," he said. "The tour won't be the same without you, but I hope you'll permit me to write to you of every detail so that you'll feel you were here in person."

Her gaze seemed to warm.

"Now," the professor continued, "if you'll allow me to make the arrangements, then help your niece pack, you won't have to worry about a thing, except to get better as quickly as possible."

Aunt Rowena patted his hand. "You're a good man, Professor. I'll leave all the arrangements to you, then. Georgina can direct you on the packing details."

Gigi wanted to protest that she didn't need help packing, but she wasn't going to turn down more time spent with the professor. It was hard to believe this was all coming to such an abrupt end. She wouldn't see Bucharest or Constantinople now, but what did that matter in the scale of what was important?

Professor Haskins turned to Gigi. "I'll be back with information soon," he said. "We should be arriving soon at the next stop, and we'll get everything settled as quickly as possible."

She followed him out into the corridor. The area was still quiet with the early hour, but she could hear the sounds of preparations coming from the dining car.

"Thank you, Professor Haskins," she said. "You certainly have a way with my aunt."

He looked like he was about to say something, but then he changed his mind. He nodded and headed down the corridor.

CHAPTER FIFTEEN

Dear Lillian,

I might arrive home before you receive this letter. You will not believe all that has happened in such a short time. Aunt Rowena has taken ill, and because of another condition that she'd kept secret from all of us, the doctor on the train has told us we need to return home at once. Professor Haskins has been wonderful and booked us on the earliest return trip. We will miss the rest of the tour, but it can't be helped. Aunt's health is more important anyway.

Irene and Blanche have decided to stay on the tour, and the professor has promised to watch over them. I'm posting this now but will write once we are en route. I wish I could explain more about Aunt Rowena, but it is not my place . . .

"Is there anything else you need, madam?" Professor Haskins asked Aunt Rowena.

She was presently tucked into her new berth on their return train, and her color had begun to return, which made Gigi feel relieved. This train was far from fully booked, and there were several empty compartments, but Gigi still felt better about sharing with her aunt.

"You have been wonderful, Professor," Aunt Rowena said, giving her best effort at a smile. "Thank you for watching over Irene and Blanche. I know they wanted to return with me, but I insisted they not throw away this trip. Georgina and I will send you letters about my progress."

"Wonderful," the professor said. "I'll look forward to hearing about every step of your recovery."

He clasped Aunt Rowena's hand, then bent to kiss her cheek.

Gigi found herself smiling but feeling teary-eyed too.

He turned to her next. "Safe travels, Miss Ballard." His voice had a new thickness to it.

"Thank you for everything." Gigi exhaled slowly. She would not cry. No.

"Care for one more stroll?" he said in a quieter voice.

Gigi's neck heated because surely her aunt had heard what the professor had said. But Rowena made no comment, so Gigi said, "I'd love to."

Professor Haskins offered his arm, and she slipped her arm through it. They left the compartment, and due to the narrow corridor, their clothing brushed as they walked together.

"Gigi, I . . ." the professor started to say, then stopped walking.

She looked up at him, so close now that she could see the green and brown in his eyes even though there wasn't full light in the corridor.

The professor drew her toward him as he stepped backward into an empty compartment that had its door open. They were out of immediate sight should anyone come into the corridor.

"I can't believe this is goodbye," the professor said.

"I can't either." Gigi gazed at this man, this kind and beautiful man who'd had his own heartbreak.

"If only . . ." He exhaled. "If only we had more time. I would have . . ."

"What?" she whispered. And then, she wasn't sure what possessed her, but she lifted her free hand and placed it on the lapel of his jacket. It was an intimate gesture to be sure, and she'd surprised herself and likely him too.

He didn't move for a moment, then he placed his warm hand over hers, bringing them even closer together. "If only we had more time," he said in a rasp, "I would have done this . . ."

Gigi's pulse had never raced so fast as it did when the professor leaned down and brushed his mouth against hers. Her fingers curled into his lapel, and she pulled him closer at the same moment he shifted his other arm about her waist. Drawing her in, he kissed her again slowly and deliberately as if he'd been thinking of this scenario before this moment.

Gigi tightened her hold on his jacket, keeping her feet from floating off the ground. It was no surprise to her that a single kiss, or three, from the professor could make her forget every man she'd ever met. For in this small train compartment, in this stolen moment, there was only him and there was only her.

The professor pulled her more fully into his arms and then buried his face against her neck.

She clung to him, knowing that this would never happen again. She'd never see him again. Never hear his voice again. This was goodbye. Her heart thumped, and she swore she could feel his thumping too.

She didn't want to let him go, but she had to. It was time.

"Clyde . . ." She felt his smile against her neck.

"I like it when you use my name, Gigi," he whispered. "And I like how you always smell like roses."

It was her turn to smile. If only they could exist in this space and moment forever. If only there weren't things and people demanding her attention. If only her aunt were healthy and they could remain on the tour.

"I'm sorry," he said, bringing her out of her reverie.

"For what?"

He lifted his head, and his gaze captured hers. The warmth and desire in his eyes was plain, sending a slow heat through her veins. "For kissing you when I shouldn't have."

She didn't want to hear this. She didn't want to have him regret anything between them.

Lifting a hand, she placed it against his cheek. "I'm glad you did. Now I have a new memory to cherish."

His gaze sobered just before he leaned down and kissed her again. This time it was brief. Like a goodbye.

"I must go, Gigi," he said, releasing her and stepping back. "I . . . I've probably confused you, and I'm sorry for that. But I wanted to kiss you just this once."

She swallowed against the pain building in her throat.

"Safe travels, dear Gigi."

She nodded, tears already trying to escape. "Safe travels, Clyde," she echoed.

And then he was gone. Just like that. Slipped into the corridor, out of her sight. She waited in the empty train compartment for several moments. After that kiss and after that goodbye, she needed to be by herself for a moment before she returned to her aunt—before she returned home to her life that would soon move on from Professor Haskins and all that they'd shared.

When the conductor called, "*En voiture!*" Gigi steeled herself to return to her compartment and begin tending to her aunt. Professor Clyde Haskins was now a thing of the past. She moved into the corridor only to nearly run into a man. For an instant, she thought it might be the professor returned to confess that he could not leave her after all, that they must find a way to be together . . .

"Nicholas," she said when she realized who the man actually was.

He nodded, his dark eyes hooded as he gazed down at her quite intently. Did she still have tears upon her cheeks? Were her eyes rimmed with red?

"You are returning home, Miss Ballard?" he said in that rich, deep voice of his.

"Yes, my aunt is following the doctor's orders," Gigi said. "Thank you for your help."

He nodded and tapped on his pipe. She thought she smelled the scent of warm chocolate—like the truffles in Vienna. But that was impossible. Regardless, the memory began to weigh her heart down again.

"You have a troubled mind," Nicholas said.

She opened her mouth to speak, but she felt a threatening sob. Instead, she brought a hand to her mouth and nodded.

"Zeh heart and mind are always connected," Nicholas said quietly. "Zey can both heal, but it takes time. Some heal more quickly zahn others." He paused. "Be patient a little longer, Miss Ballard. His heart vill soon be healed, and vehn it is, he vill come looking for you."

Gigi blinked against the stinging in her eyes and stared at Nicholas. Whatever could he mean?

Nicholas checked his pocket watch, snapped it shut, then tipped his hat. He stepped past her. Before she could ask him any questions, he strode down the corridor. Not toward the dining car, but in the opposite way. Was he getting off the train?

Gigi remained alone in the corridor for a moment, wondering what had just happened. There was only one man Nicholas could have been referring to. They had no other male acquaintance in common save for Professor Haskins. But how did Nicholas know about the depths of another person's heart? Was he some sort of fortune-teller?

Gigi had no idea what to think, but regardless of common sense or reason, Nicholas's cryptic words had given her hope where none had existed before. Still, now she must return to her aunt and push aside any foolish wishes or daydreams.

Gigi opened the compartment door and found Aunt Rowena asleep. She wasn't sweating or pale, so Gigi took that as a good sign. She adjusted the covers about her aunt, then Gigi climbed onto her own bed. If only she could sleep away the next part of the journey, then wake up in London and have her sister and mother around her to help with her aunt's recovery.

Which would mean surgery.

On one hand, Gigi understood why her aunt would put it off—surgery didn't sound like a pleasant scenario in any situation. But now Gigi worried that putting it off might make the outcome more serious. What if the delay meant her aunt's health was now in even greater peril? Should Gigi have been more insistent about returning when she'd found out in Vienna? Or should she have paid more attention to the times when Aunt Rowena had said she needed to rest?

All these regrets couldn't be helped, and Gigi knew that her aunt's stubbornness was hard to crack through. So maybe Gigi had done her best and had done all that was possible. And now she could do better with the new knowledge she had.

Gigi picked up her notebook and flipped through the most recent sketches she'd made. When she alighted on the one of men's clothing—ones that the professor had encouraged her to create—she found herself smiling and aching and missing him with a fierceness that surprised even her. The ache would diminish in time. She had to believe that.

She picked up her pencil and drew the silhouette of a man similar to the professor. His proportions were perfect for sketching. She had no photograph of him, but her memories were still fresh, and she easily filled in details of his hair and face. Next, she'd work on his clothing. Casual this time. Similar to when they'd spoken that morning on the bridge. But what could she change up? Change the color of his shirt? Add a different color thread to the seams?

Across the compartment, Aunt Rowena stirred.

Gigi immediately went on alert. "How are you feeling, Aunt?" She rose and grasped the glass of water to hand over.

Aunt Rowena's blue eyes opened. They looked clearer than they had in hours. "Is the professor gone?"

"Yes," Gigi said. "And the train has begun its journey."

"How long have I been asleep?"

"Maybe an hour."

Aunt Rowena took the glass and sipped water, then handed it back. "Write to him," she said in a soft voice. "Post it at the next stop. I have his university address written in my notebook."

"He wanted a report of your health," Gigi said. "I can wait until we arrive in London and know more."

Her aunt rested a hand on Gigi's arm. "*You* write to him. You tell him how you feel."

Gigi blinked and looked away. "I don't feel—"

"Georgina, if you don't tell him, he will never know."

"Tell him what?" She still couldn't meet her aunt's knowing gaze.

"That is for you to determine, my dear," she said. "Hearts can change, you know. Time does that, and meeting the right person who has the power to change it."

Gigi exhaled slowly. "I don't know. He has his own life. He told us both that he is a confirmed bachelor."

Aunt Rowena squeezed her arm. "It is only a letter. You will know what to say."

Perhaps she would write to him. But she would keep it informational and casual. She would thank him again for his help. What harm would that be?

CHAPTER SIXTEEN

Dear Lillian,

We just boarded the connecting train in Paris and will arrive in London soon. I likely won't post this letter, but I'm using it to write my thoughts. Aunt Rowena thinks I should write to Professor Haskins. At every stop, she insists I post something. So far I have resisted, but I am feeling those walls crumble. I've imagined many different ways to start a letter, but then I keep failing to begin.

How does one start a letter to a man whom you will never see again, yet a man who kissed you like it was the beginning of something wonderful? A kiss goodbye was what it was. A kiss for the ages. And I will never forget. What if writing to him somehow taints those last moments we had together? What if it pulls our relationship back into the ordinary, the mediocre? What if I find out that he is not who I've built him up to be? When stripped from the romantic settings and grand adventure, what if he is nothing special?

Or what if the actualization is even worse? What if I discover I've missed my one chance at finding the love of my life . . .

GIGI TORE THE LETTER IN half, then half again. Then she folded each small bit into a square. She glanced at Aunt Rowena. They were no longer in a sleeping compartment on the lavish Orient Express but sitting on rather ordinary benches. Regardless, her aunt's eyes were closed, and she was clutching her notebook to her chest. A notebook filled with more lists.

Gigi didn't know if her mother or sister would have received word in time to meet them at the station. No matter. Gigi planned to escort her aunt home,

then send word to her doctor that they'd returned and that Aunt Rowena
needed to be seen as soon as possible.

She pulled out another sheet of paper and began to write.

Dear Professor Haskins,

Scratch.

Dear Clyde,

Scratch.

Dear Professor,

Scratch.

> *Dear Professor Haskins,*
>
> *We're on our way from Paris to London. My aunt has reminded me multiple times to write, but I'm sure you aren't interested in reading about the minute details of traveling on a train. This return trip is not nearly as interesting as traveling in the tour group. I hope you are enjoying the next cities and museums.*
>
> *I will send another update when we have more news about my aunt's health. Until then, I wish you well. Once again, thank you for everything. I will cherish the memories always.*

Gigi reread the words and decided they were to the point, friendly, and
not overly taxing. He could reply or not. She'd made no mention of their shared
kiss or their private walks or anything between the two of them specifically.

Still, she wondered how she should close the letter.

Sincerely . . . In gratitude . . . Wishing you well . . . Always your friend . . .

She chose *Wishing you well*, then signed her name.

And before she could change her mind, she delivered the letter to the
conductor to post at the next stop, which would be London. She could very
well post the letter herself, but now that it was out of her hands, she couldn't
change her mind and rip up the letter.

As she headed back to her aunt's bench, there was no encounter with
Nicholas, there were no familiar voices coming from the dining car, and there
was no conversation with the professor to look forward to.

Gigi's life had shifted once again. A new slate, a new beginning, and she
must be strong for her aunt.

She hadn't expected the emotions to hit her as they did when she and
her aunt stepped off the train at the London station. They were home . . .

unexpectedly. But now, answers could be found. Her aunt could be made well.

"Gigi!" a voice called through the milling crowd.

Gigi turned at the sound of her sister's voice. "Lillian!" She laughed as her sister ran toward her. Lillian's dark hair was expertly tucked under a wide brim hat decorated in violets.

Soon, Gigi was hugging her sister. Next, Lillian hugged Aunt Rowena, albeit more gently.

"Is Mother here too?" Gigi asked.

"It's only me," Lillian told them. "We had such short notice, and Mother is preparing a room for you, Aunt Rowena."

Aunt Rowena frowned. "I'm returning to my home."

Lillian only smiled and put an arm about Aunt Rowena's shoulders. "We want you to stay with us so that we can take care of you after the surgery. It will only be for a short time, until you are well enough to get along on your own."

Gigi could see her aunt's hesitation. "I think that would be wise," Gigi added. "We can wait on you hand and foot. You can make lists and order us around."

Aunt Rowena cast her narrowed gaze upon Gigi, but there was amusement in it. "Well, this is an unexpected turn of events. I must think about it first."

Her exasperated tone didn't fool Gigi. Aunt Rowena would be giving in . . . soon.

Lillian linked her arm with their aunt's. "I've brought the carriage, and we can discuss it more on the drive to Mother's. She is hoping to see you right away. We've missed you deeply."

Aunt Rowena's face softened. "All right then. I'm not making any promises right now, mind you."

"Of course not," Lillian said with a sweet smile, then she winked at Gigi.

Gigi held back a laugh. Lillian was not only beautiful, she was also skilled in the art of persuasion. For a moment, Gigi wondered what Professor Haskins would think of her sister were he to ever meet her. Would he find her charming and beautiful? There was no secret to the fact that Lillian had the best attributes out of the two of them. Still, Gigi hoped that her friendship with the professor was solid all on its own two feet.

After they settled into the carriage and their baggage was loaded, Lillian said, "Mother has already contacted your doctor, Aunt Rowena. He'll be stopping by our house in a couple of hours."

"So soon?" Aunt Rowena said. "How ever did you manage it?"

Lillian smiled at Gigi. "I received a lot of letters. Nearly every day."

Gigi nodded, feeling pleased that she'd contributed in some small way. She couldn't explain the relief that had gone through her at the knowledge that her aunt would soon be under a doctor's care again.

The return home was a whirlwind of greeting her mother, getting Aunt Rowena settled, unpacking most of their baggage, and filling in both her mother and sister on the events of the last two days.

Aunt Rowena had fallen asleep again by the time the doctor arrived. Lillian opened the front door and brought him upstairs to the bedroom where they'd set up their aunt. Gigi was keeping vigil by her aunt's bedside, and when the doctor came in, Aunt Rowena awoke.

"I'll leave you with the doctor," Gigi said.

"No, dear," Aunt Rowena said, reaching for her hand. "Stay with me."

"Mrs. Ballard," the doctor said, walking to the other side of the bed. "I need to check the size of the growth. This might be uncomfortable."

Gigi winced along with Aunt Rowena as the doctor pressed on her abdomen.

"The good news is that the growth has not increased in size," he said. "But it has not shrunk, and you are still experiencing pain when I press in the general area. I'm also concerned about your recent illness. It might be connected, but it's impossible to tell before surgery."

Aunt Rowena blinked rapidly as if she were holding back tears.

"We can perform the surgery tomorrow," the doctor said, "and then focus on your recovery."

"Tomorrow?" Aunt Rowena blurted out. "So soon? I thought I'd have a week or two or even longer."

The doctor straightened and folded his arms. "It's already past the time that I wanted to do the surgery in the first place. No offense, ma'am, but I did not approve your travel. Since you have now returned, I see no reason for delay."

Aunt Rowena closed her eyes and exhaled. "Can you give us a moment, Doctor?"

Gigi was surprised to be included in the "us," but the doctor nodded and stepped out of the room, closing the door quietly behind himself.

Opening her eyes, Aunt Rowena looked at Gigi. "Georgina, what shall I do?"

Was her aunt truly seeking her advice on such a grave matter?

Gigi knew the right answer, but how did she suddenly have such great influence over her aunt? The woman was looking at her with an imploring expression, and Gigi realized that the time they'd spent together on the tour had brought them closer than ever. Despite the years that separated them, her aunt was now looking to Gigi for serious counsel. She took a breath, then said, "Do the surgery tomorrow. Delaying could make things more difficult, and I don't want you to have further complications."

Aunt Rowena's nod was grave. "Ask the doctor to return, my dear."

Gigi rose and crossed the room. Opening the door, she found the doctor waiting in the hallway. She motioned for him to enter, and she remained in the doorway as Aunt Rowena told him that she'd do the surgery in the morning.

After the doctor left, Gigi spent another hour by her aunt's bedside until the woman fell asleep. Once Gigi was temporarily relieved of her duties, she went into her bedroom to change into her nightdress for the evening.

Lillian waltzed in a moment later, wearing a nightdress that was more lace and ribbons than cotton fabric.

"Now," Lillian said, sitting on the edge of the bed. "You must tell me everything."

"Everything?" Gigi echoed.

Lillian batted her eyelashes. "You know, about Professor Haskins. Your dream man."

Gigi sat on the other edge of the bed. "Don't call him that. We were friends. Don't turn him into a spectacle."

Her sister's eyes rounded. "Oh. You *do* like him. I was just teasing, but now I see—"

"Don't," Gigi said. "Whether I like him or not, that doesn't signify anything. We were friends, and that is all. I'll never see him again, and I don't want my memories to have any regret in them."

"Oh, Gigi, I'm sorry. I don't mean to make light of this."

Gigi released a breath. "It is what it is. I enjoyed my time, and it was cut short, but that's how life goes sometimes." She wouldn't tell her sister about the kiss because then that would change everything.

Lillian rose and crossed to Gigi. Taking her hands, she said, "You're off duty tonight. Mother and I will check in on Aunt Rowena. She's requested that you be at the hospital with her, so we want you to get as much rest as possible."

Gigi wasn't surprised at Aunt Rowena's request, not after asking Gigi's opinion on the surgery. "All right, thank you." She watched her sister leave the room, and then she climbed into bed. At last, she could let nothingness wash over her.

CHAPTER SEVENTEEN

Dear Professor Haskins,

We arrived home safely yesterday and met with the doctor almost immediately, thanks to the arrangements by my sister and mother. By the time you receive this letter, it will all be old news, but Aunt Rowena agreed to have her surgery today. She's been out of the surgery for about two hours now and is still mostly sleeping.

Her doctor reported that she did well and that he will be sending the mass they removed to the lab for the cancer testing. So at this point, we will wait and see what the test reports bring. It's Aunt Rowena's job now to make a full recovery and my job to ensure that she does. It seems that our trip brought a new connection between the two of us, and she is wholly dependent upon me. I don't mind, although if her recovery is slow, I'll have to delay returning to work at the dressmaker's.

I hope all is well with you, and I am sure once my aunt is fully awake, she'll be asking if I've written to you yet. My answer will finally be yes.

Wishing you well,

Gigi

GIGI LOOKED AT THE WAY she'd signed her name. Was it too casual? Should she write Miss Ballard instead? Or Gigi Ballard? Or Georgina Ballard?

In the end, she left it, sealed the letter in an envelope and took it to the front reception desk at the hospital to be posted. Then she returned to her aunt's hospital room. It was a narrow room, but the tall window at one end let in plenty of light. One of the nurses had allowed Gigi to take the second bed, and now, Gigi climbed upon it to work in her sketchbook while she waited for her aunt to awaken and ask for something.

Over the next week, Gigi's routine became a series of hours of waiting for her aunt to need something. Her mother had been right to set up Aunt Rowena in their home. The recovery was slow and frustrating, but Aunt Rowena somehow stayed busy during her waking hours with making more lists, having Gigi read aloud to her, and sending out letters and notes to friends far and wide.

At the beginning of the second week, the doctor stopped in to make one of his many house calls. After checking Aunt Rowena's incision site, he declared that it was healing properly. "No activity for another two weeks at least," he said.

Aunt Rowena sighed. "I'm going stir-crazy. Is there no exception to be made?"

"No exception," the doctor said in a firm voice. "I do have news today that will cheer you up."

"Let's hear it, then," Aunt Rowena said.

"The lab tests show that the growth was cancerous, but we believe the cancer was contained to the tumor and has not spread to other locations in your body."

Gigi frowned. Was this good news? It seemed to be . . . but that still meant Aunt Rowena had had a cancerous tumor inside of her.

"Well, I suppose that's the best news I can expect," Aunt Rowena said.

"I want to see you every three months to check for any changes," the doctor added.

Aunt Rowena nodded. "Very well. Georgina will make sure I stay on task."

A bubble of pride rose in Gigi's chest.

When the doctor prepared to leave, he turned to Gigi. "Thank you for your help and all your care. Contact me with any concerns, even if your aunt wants to overlook them."

"I can hear you," Aunt Rowena chided, but her tone was amused.

The doctor nodded to Aunt Rowena. "Your determination, in all things, has served you well in the long run."

Aunt Rowena's brows lifted. "I'm taking that as a compliment, sir."

He chuckled. "As you should."

Gigi had never seen the doctor tease or laugh, and it was then she realized that doctors were very much affected by the outcome of their patients' health.

After the doctor left, Gigi crossed to her aunt to hand over a glass of water. "You're free for three months. Whatever shall we do?"

Aunt Rowena smiled. "Too bad the tour is already over, or I'd be tempted to rejoin. Perhaps we can sign up for his next one? When was it?"

"Don't even think about that right now," Gigi said with a laugh. "The doctor said two more weeks of no activity, and I intend to hold you to that."

Aunt Rowena looked up at the ceiling in mock surrender. "Maybe I should have taken your sister with me after all. She's less bossy."

Gigi only shrugged. "You wouldn't be in your second week of recovery if you had."

"True." Her aunt grasped Gigi's hand before she could step away. "Thank you, my dear. You have been my angel."

Gigi only smiled, because her throat had suddenly tightened, and she felt the familiar burning of tears.

A soft knock on the door sounded, and Gigi turned to see Lillian open it a crack. "A letter has come for you, Aunt Rowena."

"Bring it here," Aunt Rowena said immediately, her tone bright.

When Lillian handed it over, Aunt Rowena exclaimed, "Oh! It's from Professor Haskins. How wonderful." She tore at the envelope, nearly ripping it in half.

Gigi and Lillian stood together, watching their aunt. Gigi smiled at her aunt's excitement. In truth, Gigi wanted to snatch the letter and read it first. What would the professor say? He must be back at the university by now, and had likely received her avalanche of letters. What had he thought of her reports?

"Gigi," Lillian whispered, then nudged her.

Gigi looked at her sister, and Lillian pressed something against her hand. It was another letter. She glanced down at it to see it was addressed to her from the professor.

Her breath stilled, and she quickly moved her hand behind her back so that Aunt Rowena wouldn't see that there'd been a second letter from the professor. He'd written to her alone. It could be a thank-you letter, an update on the return home, maybe even a request of some sort—to keep him informed of her aunt's progress?

The rapid beating of her heart was only a reaction to the unknowns in the letter. He was a friend, and he would be writing as a friend. But in all her years, she'd never been so excited to receive correspondence from another person. She steadied her breathing as she tried to focus on Aunt Rowena while she read her letter aloud.

Gigi could barely pay attention as her aunt read. The professor thanked them for the updates, hoped that the recovery was going well, reported on the final stops of the tour, listed the museums they'd attended, and told of an amusing incident with a carriage driver who took the group to the wrong hotel.

Aunt Rowena was beaming by the time she finished reading the letter. "We must write him back immediately," she said. "He needs to know the good news."

After Lillian left, Gigi composed a return letter to the professor with the information that Aunt Rowena dictated to her.

"And tell him that after my two weeks are up, I'll be ready for another adventure."

Gigi smiled and added in that line. Then she closed off the letter.

"You must post it today," Aunt Rowena said. "I'm going to take a nap, and if I awaken before you've returned, then I'll call for Lillian."

Gigi was well-used to Aunt Rowena's demands, so this latest did not faze her at all. She was more than happy to have some time to herself because it would also allow her to read her own letter in private.

She left the bedroom and found Lillian in the drawing room absently plucking at the keys of the piano. As soon as Gigi entered, Lillian looked up in anticipation. "Well? What did your letter say?"

"I haven't read it yet," Gigi said.

"Read it now!" Lillian said with a laugh. "I can be your watchman at the door." She rose from the piano bench and crossed to the doorway, then stood as if she were a sentinel.

Gigi shook her head. "All right. All right." She crossed to the mantel, the farthest side of the room from her sister.

Opening the letter, she drew out the single sheet of paper. The first thing she noticed was that the note was short. Only a half page.

Dear Miss Ballard,

Or shall I call you Gigi? Perhaps the more formal address is better in a written letter. How are you? In your letters about your aunt, you never spoke of yourself. It's difficult to know how you are doing when I don't see you every day. I've found that I became accustomed to our talks. The rest of the tour felt different in your absence, and I think I know why.

Would it be too forward to pay you a visit? And your aunt, of course. If for no other reason than to bring good wishes to you and your family.

*If you think that would be crossing into a territory you'd
rather not enter, then at the very least, know that I wish you all
the happiness and health.*
    Sincerely,

    Clyde Haskins

Gigi had completely forgotten that she wasn't alone in the room until
Lillian spoke.

"Well, what does he say?"

Gigi looked up from the letter that she'd read three times through. "I—
He sends his good wishes. And . . . he wants to visit." Saying the words aloud
only made it more real. The professor—Clyde—had written her a letter that
was far more personal than she'd ever expected. *I think I know why . . . pay
you a visit . . . crossing into a territory . . .* She exhaled.

Then she smiled.

Lillian was grinning at her from across the room, arms folded, brown eyes
sparkling. "I think a visit would be very nice. Don't you?"

"Yes," Gigi said immediately, then laughed at her eagerness. She also
felt like crying for some reason. It was just a visit . . . and would likely be
focused on her aunt's health.

"You must write back to him," Lillian said. "Tell him that he's welcome
to visit anytime."

"Yes, I must." Gigi blinked. "I should do it now and post these letters
together."

Lillian laughed. "I agree. Do you need paper? And a pen?"

Gigi blinked again. "Yes, I do."

"I'll return shortly," Lillian said, amusement in her tone.

Lillian left the room, and Gigi reread the letter again and again. She
could hardly believe the words. They made her feel like she was back in that
empty train compartment being held by Professor Haskins. Being kissed
by him . . .

"Here you are," Lillian said, coming into the room.

Gigi took the paper and pen and sat on the settee next to the end table.
With a shaky hand, she began her reply.

Lillian pretended to ignore her and began to play the piano again—a
slow melody with plenty of crescendos and diminuendos.

Dear Professor Haskins,

You may call me Gigi in a letter. I believe our many confessions and days upon days of friendship warrant first names. Thank you for your letter. I did not expect a personal reply, but of course you may visit anytime. Aunt Rowena will be in our home for another two weeks, and then, I'm not sure if she'll want to live on her own just yet. Otherwise, you have my address, and I'd love to introduce you to my mother and sister.

Letter writing is never the same as speaking in person. And I have missed speaking to you as well. I hope you are in good health, and if the territory you mentioned is not where you want to be, I hope we can always remain friends.

Wishing you well,

Gigi

Her hand was still trembling when she addressed the envelope. Only then did she look at her sister.

Lillian stopped playing. "Well?"

"Well, I've written him back," Gigi said. "I told him he is welcome to visit anytime."

"Perfect." Lillian's smile was wide. "Now get on with you. Go post the letters."

Gigi didn't wait another moment, or she feared her nerve might leave her. Just as she opened the front door to leave the house, two women were coming up the steps. "Irene! Blanche!"

They were here to visit Aunt Rowena, of course. They visited frequently, but it was always good to see them.

"Hello, dear," Blanche said, greeting her with a kiss on the cheek. "You are smiling like a child at Christmas."

"Indeed, you are," Irene agreed, her always-observant gaze turning sharper.

"It's a beautiful day, that's all," Gigi said. "And it's wonderful to see you. My aunt will be tickled."

Blanche adjusted her rather pompous hat. "Well, if you say so. We won't keep you."

Gigi was ever grateful and left the two women staring after her. Before she turned the corner, she heard Blanche say in a rather pointed tone, "Well, if *she* won't tell us, then I know who to ask."

CHAPTER EIGHTEEN

Dear Gigi,

I hope this letter finds you well. If Sunday is available, I will come shortly after the noon hour. I'm looking forward to seeing you more than you know.
Sincerely,

Clyde

THE BACK ROOM OF THE dressmaking shop was cluttered with rolls of fabric, stacks of thread spools, and trays of beads, buttons, feathers, and other notions. Gigi was working on a series of shawls that Mrs. Stanton wanted to display for the upcoming autumn season. Gigi had decided to weave thin ribbons of browns, golds, and violets into the shawls. Working this morning was a good distraction from dwelling constantly on the professor's upcoming visit.

Today was the day. She planned to leave the shop a good hour before so that she could get home and fuss with her appearance. Gigi must remember to think of him as Professor Haskins and not Clyde. She'd reread all of his personal letters to her over and over, so she had them well memorized.

Aunt Rowena was now well enough to move about the house. She spent her mornings in the drawing room and her afternoons in the library. After that, it was an early supper and to bed for her. Gigi had gotten creative and embellished Aunt Rowena's nightdresses to cut down on the monotony of the days. Gigi had spent a portion of each day at the dressmaker's, and she'd spent off hours working on designs for men's clothing as well.

Checking the clock yet again, she realized her concentration had completely left. The professor kept entering her thoughts by way of questions of what it would be like to see him again, what their conversation might consist of. And would she see him again after this?

Mrs. Stanton came into the back room, her gray-streaked hair pulled tight into a bun. "Have you seen the peach organza?" she asked, eyeing the shawl Gigi was working on.

"It's on the top shelf there," Gigi said, nodding to the shelving on the other side of the room.

"Ah, thank you." Mrs. Stanton paused. "By the way, I wanted to speak to you for a moment. Frederica just turned in her notice. I can hire another shop girl, or you could work more hours."

Frederica worked with the wealthier clients one-on-one. She had a great eye for fashion, but she was also flakey and usually showed up late.

"Why is she leaving?"

Mrs. Stanton pursed her lips. "She says she's been hired for more money at Bovine's Millenary."

A sore point to be sure, since Mrs. Stanton and Mrs. Bovine competed for some of the same customers. Mrs. Stanton had started selling hats, and Mrs. Bovine had started offering alterations and ready-made clothing. But if Gigi were to do Frederica's job in catering to the customers, then she wouldn't be hands-on with the clothing anymore.

"Can I think about it and let you know tomorrow?"

"Of course." Mrs. Stanton took down the organza, then went back into the front of the shop.

Gigi sighed. She was even more distracted now, and she might as well call it a day, then come back fresh tomorrow with her decision, whatever that might be . . .

Once she made the short walk home, she walked into a flower-laced drawing room. Apparently, Aunt Rowena had ordered half the flowers in London to be delivered to their home.

"What's this?" Gigi asked, turning to survey the drawing room. "Are you turning this into a garden?"

Aunt Rowena chuckled from her spot by the hearth, which had been lit, even though it was the middle of summer. Since her surgery, she complained about always being cold.

"It's an added welcome for the professor," Aunt Rowena said. "We used to discuss types of flowers. Apparently his mother won many contests for best roses. Did he not tell you?"

"No," Gigi said. She moved about the room, examining a few of the arrangements. "But so many?"

"If it can't be done well, then why do it at all?" her mother said, coming into the room.

Her mother wore one of her best day dresses and had obviously taken time to fix her hair. Lillian was right on their mother's heels. She looked beautiful in a soft-pink dress with ruffles at the neck and wrists.

Gigi looked down at her work skirt and blouse that had seen better days. "I should go change."

"You should," Lillian said brightly.

Her mother just smiled, and Aunt Rowena seemed distracted by checking something in her notebook.

Gigi went up the stairs to her bedroom. Noon would arrive in a half hour, and then the professor would be here unless he was delayed by something. Would he be on time? Would he come at all? Of course he was coming . . . She changed into a fresh blouse and a dark-green skirt. She didn't want to dress up too much or look like she was trying too hard. And yet . . .

By the time she'd brushed out her hair, then pinned it and repinned it, the time was dangerously close to noon.

She could hear the voices of her family downstairs, and she knew she should hurry down. But she was glued to her bedroom window that overlooked the street, watching for any sign of the professor. She studied the passing carriages and analyzed the pedestrians.

The appointed time came and went. Five minutes, then ten minutes. A carriage slowed on the opposite side of the street, and out stepped a man she'd recognize in any country. Professor Haskins was here—at her home! She watched him walk across the street, coming closer. His jacket was a deep brown, and she knew instinctively that it would make his eyes more brown when she saw him up close.

His pale-blond hair beneath his hat seemed shorter than when she'd last seen him, and his stride was sure and confident.

She still hadn't moved from the window.

When a knock sounded at the door, she nearly jumped. She needed to go downstairs now.

After taking a deep breath and smoothing her palms over her skirt, she left her bedroom. The voices coming from the drawing room were female mixed with a familiar male voice. Gigi quickened her step and pushed herself to keep moving even though her heart was already in her throat.

"Wonderful to meet you," her mother's voice rang out. "We've heard so much about you, and we appreciate your care and concern for my sister-in-law."

The professor murmured something that Gigi couldn't quite make out. She stepped into the drawing room. His back was to her as he faced her aunt.

"You are looking lovely, ma'am," he said, and it wasn't any surprise that a flush stole over Aunt Rowena's cheeks as she gazed up at him.

"Thank you for coming, Professor," Aunt Rowena said. "I hope you plan to stay for a while because I want to hear all about the rest of the tour. I almost invited Irene and Blanche over for a little reunion but perhaps next time. I'd rather have you all to myself."

The professor laughed, and the warmth reached across the room and sent Gigi's pulse thrumming.

"I have many stories to tell," he said, the timbre of his voice low, so familiar yet so new at the same time.

And then he turned, and their gazes connected. Warmth skittered across Gigi's skin, and her chest felt like she'd exhaled after holding her breath for many moments.

All the greetings Gigi had planned to say flew right out of her mind.

"Hello, Miss Ballard," the professor said, his gaze intent, his words even more intent.

Lillian nudged her, and Gigi managed to say, "Welcome, Professor." Such a profound statement, she thought with a grimace. That was all she'd come up with?

Professor Haskins's gaze didn't miss a thing, and she felt as if he was seeing all of her at once, both inside and out. His mouth curved into a smile, and he gave her a small nod . . . Had he winked?

She wasn't entirely sure because she felt like she was in some sort of strange dream seeing the professor in her family drawing room in the space where she spent part of every day.

"Have a seat," her mother said. "I'll have our maid bring in tea. I assume you'd like some refreshment."

"I've never turned down refreshment," he said with a smile.

Everyone laughed, or giggled, making the drawing room sound like a children's schoolyard.

Gigi's face warmed. Her family sure acted differently when there was a gentleman in the room.

"Tell me all about how your recovery is going," the professor asked her aunt.

So they sat through several moments of Aunt Rowena's update. The tea arrived, and her mother poured a cup for everyone after asking the professor how he liked his tea.

"One sugar."

Had he looked at Gigi on purpose when he spoke? Why was she reading so much into his every word and action?

"Now, tell us all about the rest of the tour," Aunt Rowena said. "I must live vicariously through you."

The professor chuckled. "If you must know, the tour was not the same without the two of you." His gaze slid to Gigi's.

And of course Lillian was watching her closely, a sly smile on her face, probably checking for any reactions. Gigi was sure she'd get an earful after the professor left.

She wasn't even sure she absorbed any of his descriptions of the cities, hotels, and museums. She was certainly looking at him, listening even, just not exactly comprehending.

"And now what are your plans?" Aunt Rowena said.

"I'm preparing for my next round of lectures at the university," he said. "Classes begin in a few weeks."

"Ah, so you have a bit of a break."

His smile turned amused. "A bit."

"Perfect," Aunt Rowena said. "That means you should accompany us to the Victoria and Albert Museum in two weeks' time. That will be my first outing, and I've never attended with an art expert."

This was quite a bold invitation, and Gigi tried to act like she wasn't surprised at her aunt's request. Having the professor pay a short visit and politely inquire after her health was one thing . . . but inviting him on an outing was quite another.

"I'd love to," he said with no hesitation.

Aunt Rowena clasped her hands together. "Wonderful."

Without even meeting her aunt's gaze, Gigi knew that the invitation had been for *her* benefit. Her aunt hadn't given up. Not yet. Gigi wanted to laugh. Her aunt might have asked for forgiveness in her matchmaking schemes, but she could not truly change her character.

"I thank you for the refreshments," the professor said. "And it was great to meet everyone."

"Thank you for your visit," Aunt Rowena said. "You have been a kind man, and I will recommend your tour to everyone I know."

"Very well," he said in an amused tone.

Everyone but Aunt Rowena rose as he stood, and it was like a crew of sparrows following him to the door.

He took his hat from the coat rack and turned a final time. At least what Gigi had thought was a final time.

"Miss Ballard," he said, his gaze upon her. "Would you care to go for a stroll?"

She was stunned, to say the least. He'd asked her to go for a walk in front of her entire family . . . Of course, it wasn't like they would have a chance to be alone on their walk. Not like those stolen moments on the train.

"Yes," she said, knowing she sounded breathless. "I'd like that very much."

Lillian was probably about to laugh, and her mother was beaming. Surely Aunt Rowena could hear them from the drawing room and was likely silently clapping.

"I'll just get my hat."

"Oh, you can wear mine," Lillian said, plucking her hat from the coat rack, where she must have left it earlier.

"All right." Gigi exhaled and put on the hat, her fingers trembling.

Lillian moved close to help her pin it in place.

"Thank you," Gigi said, her face heating up.

Lillian only smiled. "Have a nice walk."

Professor Haskins . . . Clyde . . . opened the door, and she stepped out first. The day was rather warm, but Gigi didn't mind in the least. He extended his arm, and just like that, they were walking side by side along her neighborhood street.

She couldn't think of a thing to say, and she doubted her voice would be steady anyway.

The professor didn't say anything for a long moment either, and perhaps that was all right. But as the silence stretched, Gigi began to feel antsy.

"Thank you again for coming," she said. "My aunt has been looking forward to this for a long time . . . really, since we left the tour."

He slowed their steps. "And you?"

The two words were simple but said so much.

She looked up at him to find his gaze on her, open and steady.

"You know I've been looking forward to seeing you."

He smiled. "That's good to hear." Then he fully stopped, bringing her to a stop as well. They'd reached the edge of a small park. Children were playing beyond, watched over by nurses or mothers.

"Gigi . . ." He released her arm and took her hand. "I didn't know how it would be seeing you again. I wondered if the enjoyment I found in spending time with you was part of the nature of the tour. But when you walked into the drawing room earlier today, I knew it wasn't just the tour."

She had to look away from his penetrating gaze, so she looked down at their linked hands instead as his thumb skimmed over her wrist. Her heart was nearing double-time, and she wasn't even sure she could take a full breath.

"Gigi . . ."

She lifted her chin and saw a tenderness in his gaze that sent hope skittering throughout her body.

"May I court you?"

Her eyes began to burn. Why would she cry now? She should be happy. But she *was* happy, she realized, and apparently that was going to make her cry. "Yes," she whispered because that was all she could manage for now.

"Do you need my handkerchief?" he asked.

She nodded. "I think I do."

His mouth curved into a smile as he handed it over. Gigi dabbed at her eyes, then inhaled. "I'm sorry. I don't know what's wrong with me. I guess I thought you were set on being a bachelor as you told me—"

His hand touched her jaw, effectively stopping her speech. "I know what I said, and it was true at the time that I spoke the words. But when you left the tour, I was at a loss . . . a feeling I'd never had before. I knew it was because you weren't with me."

She blinked back new tears. "So that kiss wasn't a goodbye?"

His eyes danced with merriment, and he dropped his hand to grasp her other hand. "Not at all. It was a beginning." He tilted his head. "If that's all right with you."

"It's all right with me."

The professor smiled, and he squeezed her hand. "If only we weren't in a public place . . ." His voice trailed off, but the meaning was clear in his eyes.

She wanted to kiss him too. Instead, she smiled. Had she ever smiled so much around a single person? She highly doubted it. "I'm guessing you'll come to the museum with us in two weeks. My aunt is so looking forward to it."

"I can't wait two weeks before seeing you again," he said. "It must be much sooner. Maybe tomorrow."

Her heart leapt at this declaration. "Tomorrow might set my family all atwitter."

"I don't mind," he said in a low voice that sent a delicious shiver through her.

She wanted to grin, but she kept her calm as she said, "How about the day after? We could walk in the park. I'll keep my afternoon free." She pushed away the thoughts of how Mrs. Stanton wanted her to work extra hours. Because Professor Haskins wanted to see her again.

"It's a plan," he said. "What time shall I be at your place?"

Would it be childish to skip all the way home? It was impossible to keep a smile at bay. Did she look overeager? And was she really having this conversation with Professor Haskins? It appeared so. He still had a hold of her hands, and the depths of his hazel eyes were focused solely on her. "Three o'clock?"

He nodded. "I'll be there."

It seemed dreams really could come true. And now she was reluctant to return home, but she knew their time was short if they were to keep things proper.

As if reading her thoughts, he said, "I should walk you back home or your family will think I've spirited you away."

As they walked back, she said, "What sort of lectures are you preparing, Professor Has—?"

"Clyde, my dear Gigi," he said. "Please call me Clyde."

Surely she was blushing now. "What sort of lectures are you preparing, Clyde?"

He grinned. "Interesting that you should ask. I'm preparing a presentation on Johann Friedrich Overbeck."

"Ah." Warmth prickled her skin. "Does one have to be a university student to hear your lectures?"

"For some, yes," he said. "But there are other special-occasion lectures that are open to the public."

They'd reached her home, and his steps slowed as he gazed down at her. "Would you like to be my guest?"

She stopped with him, lifting her chin. "I would."

"Excellent."

They stood for a moment, the traffic in the street a distant sound, the warm breeze stirring their clothing as a new understanding formed between them.

She wanted to step into his arms, to nestle against him, to have him lean down and . . .

"Come," he said in a quiet voice. "I'm fairly certain your sister or mother just parted the drapes to make sure we are being proper."

Gigi laughed. Hope had lodged itself firmly inside of her. Clyde Haskins was a fine man indeed. Handsome and kind and tempting all in one breath. And she was falling quite madly, deeply, and completely in love with him.

CHAPTER NINETEEN

Dear Clyde,

It feels strange to write your first name, and I almost wrote Professor Haskins. But I am being obedient to your wishes. You were right. My sister was peering through the drapes, spying on us. Although she denied it, I know my sister almost better than myself.

I'm afraid that when you show up tomorrow afternoon, you'll be facing a barrage of women again. My mother, my aunt, and my sister are fully invested in you courting me. I hope it wasn't too forward of me to tell them that bit at least. If so, then it's too late now to take back that revelation. Otherwise, I will plan to apologize properly. Preferably in private . . .

THE LETTER WAS POSTED, AND her flirtatious words played in her mind as Gigi walked from the post to the dressmaker's shop. She'd been keeping herself as busy as possible—attending to Aunt Rowena, even though she was nearly back to full health, drawing up various sketches for her sister's wedding dress, working on her men's fashions. But . . . her mind strayed most often to Clyde.

Was he truly denouncing his bachelorhood? For her?

The idea was a heady one, that she was the woman to bring such a charming man back into availability.

She spent part of the day helping a few of the clients in Frederica's place at the dressmaker's shop. It wasn't as bad as she thought it might be, although the customers were definitely pretentious. At least Gigi knew what to recommend.

She'd finished with her last client and was straightening things in the shop when Lillian came in.

Alarm shot through Gigi immediately as she wondered if something was wrong with Aunt Rowena. Had there been a setback? But Lillian was all smiles. "I thought you might want to see this sooner than later." She waved an envelope.

It had to be from Professor Haskins—Clyde—or why else would her sister tease her?

She snatched the letter, unable to hide her impatience.

Lillian laughed as she released it. "Now that I've brought it all the way over here, you'd better tell me what it says."

Glancing at Mrs. Stanton, who seemed preoccupied with the accounting ledgers, Gigi motioned for her sister to follow her into the back room.

She tore open the letter with little ceremony and couldn't help but skim the words quickly before reading more slowly. But it wasn't a note of flowery sentiments or sweet promises. No . . . Her chest went tight.

"What is it?" Lillian asked, her tone concerned.

"It's . . ." Gigi swallowed. "Here. Read it yourself." She closed her eyes, unable to watch how her sister's expression might change.

> *Dear Miss Ballard,*
>
> *I have some news, and we must speak in person. Unfortunately, something from my past has arisen. I won't be able to make our arranged time tomorrow. How does the following afternoon sound?*
> *Sincerely,*
>
> *Professor Haskins*

"What does this mean?" Lillian asked.

Gigi opened her eyes. "I'm not exactly sure, but whatever it is, it's not good."

Her sister frowned. "How can you be sure? It's not exactly a set down."

Her breath was turning shallow. "He called me Miss Ballard and signed it Professor Haskins."

Lillian's mouth formed an *O*. "Ah. I see." She folded the letter. "And you think that's significant?"

By the growing hollow in her stomach, Gigi had no doubt. "Yes. The last time we saw each other, he was insistent that I call him Clyde. He's been calling me Gigi since . . . since Vienna."

Lillian nodded as if she understood perfectly. "I see. Well . . ." She exhaled. "I suppose we'll have to wait until tomorrow to find out. There's nothing you can do right now personally."

"Except worry," Gigi said in a dull voice.

"Except that." Lillian stepped close to Gigi and slipped an arm around her shoulders. "You'll face this like the strong woman you are. Whatever it is, it's not something *you've* done wrong. He did say this thing was from his past."

Gigi leaned into her sister. "That's what worries me the most."

Lillian rubbed Gigi's shoulder. "Why?"

"He was engaged before," she said. "Did I tell you that?" She pressed on without waiting for a reply. "The breakup was so devastating to him that he didn't want to marry ever."

"But you've changed that already," Lillian said. "So maybe it's something else with his family. What is his family like?"

"He hasn't really talked about them," Gigi said with a sigh. "What if I don't know him at all? What if there are secrets in his past or—"

"Shh," Lillian soothed. "You can worry yourself sick, or you can reconcile yourself to supporting him in whatever predicament he's found himself. Perhaps it's something that he's worried will put you off. So now you need to decide how you truly feel about him."

Gigi nodded, hoping her sister was right . . . that this was something that he was just worried about and not something that would return him to his bachelor status.

"Tonight you will be sufficiently distracted," Lillian continued. "Bart and his family are coming for supper, remember?"

This only made Gigi feel worse. She could already feel her mood shifting to pensive, and now she'd have to be around company who'd only want to talk about the upcoming wedding plans for Lillian and Bart, the perfect couple.

"Can you leave work a little early?" Lillian said. "I'll buy you an ice. I feel terrible for bringing you a letter that has you so worried."

Gigi bit her lip. "I suppose I can leave a little early, but you shouldn't feel guilty. None of this is your doing."

"I'm sorry all the same," Lillian said in a soft voice, then moved to hug Gigi.

Gigi squeezed her sister tight. If nothing else, she had her family. And now Aunt Rowena was nearly as good as new.

The two sisters made their way down the street in the sunny afternoon. Carts and carriages rolled by, and pedestrians bustled about their business. Everyone seemed to have a purpose, an errand, and no one seemed to be sinking into themselves like Gigi was. She would get through this. Her sister was right. Whatever it was, Gigi would be strong.

But curiosity continued to burn hot in her chest throughout the evening as she prepared for the supper and as she greeted their guests.

Bart was a good match for Lillian in more ways than one. His dark hair and brown eyes complemented Lillian's nearly black hair and lighter brown eyes. But Bart indulged in Lillian's chatter, and no matter what she said, he seemed enamored of her. Their favorite thing was to escape to the back garden, where Bart always plucked her a flower. His father, Mr. Anderson, was the quiet sort, and Mrs. Anderson was instantly in cahoots with Aunt Rowena as they discussed wedding flowers. Gigi tried to join in with the supper conversation, but she couldn't focus. All she could think about was Clyde's letter.

She'd read it through a second time when she was dressing for tonight's supper, and the feeling of foreboding had swept over her again.

By the time the evening ended and the Anderson family had gone home, Gigi felt like she would never calm down enough to sleep. She retired as soon as she could, but she still lay in her dark bedroom, gazing at the sliver of moonlight coming through the drapes.

Finally, she climbed out of bed, pulled on a robe, and began to write a letter she'd never send.

Dear Professor Haskins,

I understand that sometimes life doesn't fall into line how we plan. Our first plan is thwarted, and our second plan is as well. I can only guess at what complications you are facing right now, but if my guess is right, please know you don't owe me anything, not even an explanation, although it would be nice to have it. You can write me back with any message you need to convey, and I will understand your reluctance and distance.

We began as friends, and I hope we might remain friends.
Sincerely,

Miss Ballard

Gigi gazed at the letter for several long moments. Maybe she could post it first thing in the morning and be done with this situation once and for all. Or she could rip up the letter and face the professor in person. Would it be harder to do so? To see him one more time? To remind herself of what she was losing?

She folded the letter and slipped it into the pocket of her robe. She'd speak to her aunt and then decide. Gigi headed to Aunt Rowena's room. Thankfully a light spilled under the door, and Gigi hoped that meant her aunt was awake reading. Gigi tapped softly on the door, then turned the doorknob. Entering the room, she found Aunt Rowena propped against her pillow, a notebook in hand.

"You're still up, dear?" Aunt Rowena said. "I thought everyone had gone to sleep—the best time for me to make my lists without any interruptions."

Gigi edged farther into the room. "What list are you making now?"

"Oh, it's the one for our museum trip with the professor." Aunt Rowena smiled, then her smile dropped. "What's the matter? And don't tell me you're fine; I can see you're troubled."

Gigi perched on the edge of the chair nearest her aunt's bedside table. "I received a letter from the professor today, and I don't know what to make of it."

Aunt Rowena's brows rose. "What does it say?"

Gigi pulled the folded letter from her pocket. "Read it. I don't mind."

Her aunt took the letter, opened it, then read the short note. "Ah."

When she said nothing more, Gigi said, "What do you think it means?"

Lips pursed, Aunt Rowena folded the letter carefully, then handed it back. "I believe it is something to do with the woman he was engaged to. Olivia? Was that her name? Otherwise, what news could affect anything between the two of you?"

Gigi felt like her heart had dropped to her stomach. "That's my guess as well."

"I'm sorry, my dear," Aunt Rowena said. "But if he's not completely loyal to you by now, it might be just as well."

Gigi hated her aunt's conclusion, but she was also right.

Aunt Rowena extended her hand, and Gigi reached out to grasp it. "You are a fine woman, my dear. Be proud of your accomplishments and the way you've lived your life. Don't let another person's decisions or preferences determine your own worth."

"Thank you," Gigi whispered and rose to kiss her aunt's cheek.

Eventually Gigi would know what the professor needed to speak to her about, and only then could she make her next decision. She returned to her bedroom and ripped up the letter.

CHAPTER TWENTY

Since both Lillian and Aunt Rowena knew of the professor's letter, Gigi had told her mother as well. And that was why she was currently sitting on a bench in the park, awaiting his arrival. She'd told her family that this was no ordinary visit, and since it wasn't likely filled with good news, she didn't want to go through the farce of everyone greeting him again at the house.

So her family was under strict instructions to tell him where to find her. Aunt Rowena offered to give him a stern talking-to, but Gigi had immediately negated that idea.

The day had been warm, but clouds had raced across the sky about an hour ago and now had taken up residence over London. It was fitting that the temperature should drop, and now she wished she'd brought a jacket or shawl. The cool wind had brought out people with kites to the park. Gigi watched the children run about with their contraptions, calling to each other, laughing in their play.

It all made her feel even more lonely. Her sister would be married soon. Her aunt would return to her home. Her mother would continue in the busyness of her social circles. And Gigi would return to the dressmaker's shop, day in and day out, surrounded by people yet lonely all the same.

The footsteps that approached every so often invariably passed her by and moved on. She didn't think the professor would be late, or at least not very late, but as the moments passed, she felt the absence keenly. What if he'd changed his mind? What if he'd been delayed? What if he'd decided to send a note of explanation after all?

Another set of footsteps approached, but Gigi didn't even look up until someone sat next to her on the bench.

The man wore dark trousers, and she immediately recognized the leather shoes of the professor.

She looked up to see his hazel eyes on her. She felt a physical jolt as their eyes met because there was not the usual warmth in his but a wariness . . . and a regret?

"Your mother told me I would find you here," he said.

"I hoped you'd remember where the park was."

"I did." He gave her a small smile, and he seemed to be studying her face. "Thank you for agreeing to change our meeting time."

His words felt so formal, stilted, and almost forced. She wanted to turn back the clock to his first visit, when they'd laughed together and couldn't stop smiling at each other. But this man was somber to say the least.

"You're welcome," she said in a quiet voice. "I've been worried about you."

His brows lifted. "You have?"

She looked down at her lap because she could feel the emotion pushing through unbidden. "I hate to think that you are troubled or that you might be in any sort of pain."

He said nothing for a long moment.

The sounds about the park seemed to fade, and the wind turned even colder. She tried not to shiver, but it was impossible now. The temperature had dropped too much.

"You are cold," he murmured, and before she could protest, he'd shrugged out of his jacket and set it over her shoulders.

The warmth was immediate. Whether it was from the heavy fabric or the knowledge of who the jacket belonged to, she wasn't sure. His scent of woodsy soap seemed to surround her like a caress. But it couldn't last long; that she knew. She'd seen the regret in the professor's gaze already. This meeting was a goodbye.

"Miss Ballard," he said, "you're a remarkable woman."

He hadn't called her Gigi, and she knew that was significant. She pulled the jacket closer, for it might be her last chance to breathe in the familiarity of his scent.

"I'm sorry you felt you had to come all this way to . . ." Her voice broke off in a choke. She didn't want to cry now. He'd come to tell her something, and she should be woman enough to listen without melting into a weeping puddle.

"I've brought something for you to read," he said. "At first, I was stunned when I received this letter. I didn't believe a word of it. But I realized I was being a hypocrite if I couldn't allow another person to change his ways . . . or her ways."

Gigi's chin lifted at the mention of *her*. "Is it from Olivia?"

The professor's brows shot up. "How did you know?"

Gigi's smile was bitter. "I couldn't think of anything else that would come between . . . us."

His gaze fell then, and his eyes slowly closed.

The tears couldn't be held back any longer, and Gigi fished out a handkerchief from her bag. Ironically, it was the first one he'd given her. Now, she supposed she should give it back.

The professor reached inside his vest pocket and brought out a letter. He handed it over, and Gigi took it. She wanted to rip it up. Stomp on it. Even burn it. Instead, she sniffled and began to read the words.

Dear Clyde,

It has been too long since we spoke those bitter words to each other. I have apologized to you a thousand times in my mind, perhaps more. I could say that I was not myself, but that wouldn't be true. I was a version of myself that I have since grown to detest. You were right. There was another man, although I could not admit it to you at the time.

We did marry, you see, but now . . . he has left. That is not the worst of it though. He has divorced me, so not only am I an abandoned woman, but I am a fallen woman. The human spirit is surprisingly strong, though, and I have done everything to pull myself back onto my feet. I've found a job as a typist. I know you must be laughing by now at a menial job I always snubbed my nose at. Telling you that I wanted to be a society wife like my mother and her mother before her was perhaps the most foolish thing I've ever said. Among other things.

Bless you if you're still reading this missive. I wouldn't have ever written you if I didn't regret our canceled engagement. You are a good man, a kind man, and someone I didn't appreciate when I should have. I let myself be blinded by foolish dreams. The reality is that I've never forgotten you or what we shared. You are my best memories, dear Clyde.

If nothing else, I'd love to speak to you and apologize properly.
It would give me the much-needed peace I am craving, and I hope
it will bring you peace and closure as well.
Lovingly,

Olivia

After reading the letter, Gigi dabbed at the tears on her cheeks. The letter by itself wasn't as fearsome as she thought it might be. In fact, she was happy Clyde had received the apology he needed. But what had the professor decided to do?

"I met with her last night," he said in a quiet tone. "She is much changed."

Gigi held her breath. She couldn't look at Clyde because she didn't want to see the light in his eyes as he spoke of Olivia.

"She apologized, quite a bit, in truth," he said. "And she . . . she wants a reconciliation."

Now, Gigi looked at the professor. "How can she ask that? After all this time? She's returning to you *after* breaking your heart and *after* the man she chose divorced her." She hadn't meant to burst out with her argument, but now there was no taking it back. And she wasn't done. She handed back the letter. "It's a pretty apology to be sure, but what about *you*? Are you supposed to forget all about what she put you through? Not only forgive and forget but take her back? Trust her again?"

His gaze was steady, his jaw set firm, and Gigi had a terrible feeling that he'd already . . . accepted her? Taken her back? Had he loved her so much that he was willing to work through betrayal of the worst kind?

Curse this man and his good nature. Because of it, Gigi was now out in the cold, both literally and figuratively.

But her aunt's words came back to her mind from the previous night. The letter from Olivia was the ultimate test of where Clyde Haskins's loyalties lay. And they were certainly not with her.

"Miss Ballard."

Gigi was furious. He had no right to reduce her to *Miss Ballard* after all that had happened, after all that they'd shared, including their letters that had grown increasingly more intimate. She was done. She wasn't going to sit there while he explained away how letting Olivia back into his life would be in any way a good idea.

It was a terrible idea.

But just like the wind now knifing through her clothing and hair, she felt like the professor might as well have just taken out her heart and stomped on it.

She stood abruptly. She shrugged off the jacket and set it on the bench. Then she fled the park and headed toward home.

She thought she heard him calling after her, but it was likely the wind. The wind that now tugged at her clothing and hair so that by the time she reached home, she was a frightful mess.

Her family was waiting in the drawing room, and Irene and Blanche were visiting. Gigi paused there for only a moment to see all eyes turned upon her in anticipation.

Gigi exhaled a slow breath. "He received a letter from her." She didn't need to define "he" or "her." And she knew that Irene and Blanche had been kept up-to-date by Aunt Rowena. "She wants to reconcile, and he's considering it." Her voice faltered, and instead of losing her composure—what little she had left—she hurried to the stairs, then headed to her room.

She walked into her room, and with trembling hands, she unfastened her hat, then took out the pins in her hair. Next came her shoes and blouse and skirt. Finally she crawled into bed and hugged a pillow against her chest. She wanted this day to be over with. This week. This month. This entire summer. She wanted to erase Clyde Haskins from her memories and thoughts completely.

Because it hurt so much.

She hadn't even allowed herself to hope until recently, until he told her he was ready to put the past behind him.

The pain came from knowing that Clyde Haskins was such a good man, an honest man, that he'd take back a woman who'd hurt him so thoroughly. That perhaps he still loved her enough to do that. If it had only been pity, then Clyde Haskins would have chosen Gigi.

But he hadn't.

The tears came again, hot and fast this time, soaking unheeded into her pillow and hair. She didn't sob. No, they were silent tears.

Throughout the next couple of hours, different members of her family came into her room. First, her mother, who sat by her bed and stroked her hair, saying nothing.

Then, Aunt Rowena came in with her slower, shuffling step. She pulled a chair close to Gigi's bed and took her hand.

"I have written the professor several scathing letters," Aunt Rowena said. "I haven't decided which to send yet. Maybe all of them."

Gigi couldn't help but smile at her aunt's pronouncement, but then the tears started again. She closed her eyes against the pain, but it did nothing to ease it. The memories were all still there in her mind, vivid and real.

Aunt Rowena patted her hand. "Tomorrow is another day. It will be a better day, I assure you, my dear."

Because nothing can top the news of today, Gigi thought, but she didn't say the words aloud. The bitterness would come later, she was sure. Right now, the pain was numbing. She tightened her hand around her aunt's. Gigi thought of the things she was grateful for and would always be grateful for: Her aunt's recovering health. Her sister having a man who loved her and would marry her. Her mother's stalwart determination.

Heartbreaks happened in life. They couldn't be avoided. But why, oh why, had she allowed herself to fall in love with him?

CHAPTER TWENTY-ONE

Dear Miss Ballard,
Dear Miss Ballard,
Dear Miss Ballard,

THE LETTERS HAD CURLED INTO flames inside the hearth, the words turning black before Gigi could read them, until only the opening line was visible for a half second. Soon that, too, turned to ash.

The professor had written three times.

Gigi had burned each one of his letters. There was nothing to be said. Nothing to be sorry for. He had his love back, and Gigi had to begin anew.

Two weeks had passed since the arrival of the first three letters, and now it appeared they'd all stopped. A relief to be sure, but as Gigi returned home each afternoon from the dressmaker's, she found herself disappointed to not have anything addressed to her in the post.

It seemed today was another day with no letter.

"You're back early," Lillian exclaimed from the drawing room, where she and Aunt Rowena were sorting through a basket of ribbons—most likely something to do with the wedding. Her mother sat close to the hearth's warmth since it was a blustery day outside.

"Mrs. Stanton is hosting a dinner tonight," Gigi said, walking into the drawing room, "so we locked up a little early." She paused when she saw that Irene and Blanche were both visiting.

"Hello, dear," Blanche said. She was bedecked in a deep-green dress with matching emerald jewelry.

"You are just in time," Irene added. "Your sister is in dire need of your help."

Irene and Blanche visited every few days, and Aunt Rowena was always delighted to see them.

Gigi sat in the chair across from Lillian and Aunt Rowena. "What have you got there?"

"Well, we're making a mess of things," Aunt Rowena said. "I told your sister we should wait until you returned."

Lillian sighed. "I can't *always* depend on Gigi. I've got to be able to do some things on my own." But the smile she gave Gigi told her that they'd been waiting for her.

"We're picking out the ribbons for wrapping the posies we'll give to all the wedding guests. But I can't decide between the lavender and the green."

"Ah." Gigi tilted her head as her sister held up both ribbons. "How about both colors?"

"Both?"

Gigi crossed to the women, took the two ribbons from Lillian, and intertwined them around the posy they were using as a sample. She tied a neat bow, then clipped the ends of the ribbon. Holding it up, she smiled. "I like it. What do you think?"

Aunt Rowena clapped. "Perfect! What did I tell you, Lillian?"

Lillian rolled her eyes good-naturedly.

"I'm the one who told Lillian that she needed to wait for Georgina," Irene said.

"It doesn't matter who said what," Blanche cut in.

Their mother said, "I second the vote, if we are voting, that is."

"All right, all right," Lillian said, rising and curtsying to Gigi. "You are officially crowned queen of all decorations and fashions."

"Why thank you." Gigi laughed. It felt good to laugh, and she needed to do more of it.

The doorbell rang, and everyone in the room stilled.

"Are you expecting someone, Hester?" Aunt Rowena asked their mother.

"Not at all," she said, a frown marking her brow.

"Perhaps it's that handsome Bart?" Irene suggested.

They all waited as Mr. Carson took his time walking to the door. When it opened, they listened for the sound of voices.

The person at the door sounded like a young boy . . .

Moments later, Mr. Carson appeared in the doorway of the drawing room. "A delivery for Miss Ballard."

Of course, that could mean either Gigi or Lillian, and Lillian swept over to accept the package. "Something from Bart?" she said to no one in particular.

"What a thoughtful young man," Blanche said in a dreamy voice.

"I'll say," Irene agreed.

Gigi returned to fiddling with the ribbons and the posy.

"Oh, it's addressed to Miss *Georgina* Ballard," Lillian pronounced.

Gigi lifted her head. "Who would send *me* something?" She couldn't think of a single soul. "What's the return address?"

Lillian pursed her lips and handed over the package. "You can see for yourself."

Gigi took the package, her breath already shortened. When she saw the name of Clyde Haskins for the return address, she nearly dropped the package. "Professor Haskins," she murmured, feeling all eyes upon her. Perhaps she should just throw it in the fire or return it without opening it. But truthfully, her curiosity was burning a hole in her chest.

Besides, her family and guests were waiting in anticipation.

She turned the package and tugged at the brown paper outer wrapping. She tried not to think how, just a short time ago, the professor had been sealing up this package for her. It didn't weigh much, and she wondered what could weigh so little. Had she forgotten something on the train, and he'd packed it up?

Another box sat inside the first box. This one was covered in cloth and was decidedly foreign, but she couldn't place the origin.

She glanced at Aunt Rowena, but the wrinkle in her brow indicated that she didn't have any ideas either.

Lillian leaned forward from where she sat. "Well, hurry up, sister."

Gigi smirked, if only to cover up the nervous staccato of her heartbeat. She lifted the lid of the second box. There, nestled in tissue paper, was a small teacup. Gigi instantly knew which shop it was from and where exactly in Vienna.

This teacup would be a pretty complement to the one she'd picked out while she and Professor Haskins had been in the toy shop. He must have purchased it on the return trip.

"A single teacup?" Aunt Rowena frowned. "Whatever can the professor mean by that?"

"Goodness," Blanche said. "It's quite lovely, for what it's worth."

"Who would send anyone a single teacup?" Irene asked.

Gigi had only told Lillian about the teacups she'd decided to start collecting. The experience now seemed like it was another lifetime ago. She lifted the delicate china from its nest and turned it to catch the light. The porcelain was fine, and the painted violet was delicate handiwork.

She loved it.

"Oh, there's a note," Lillian said. "Shall we burn it?"

Not many secrets were kept in this household.

"Why would anyone burn a note?" Irene asked.

"Hush," Blanche said.

Gigi looked down at the box again. Sure enough, a card poked out from beneath the tissue paper. She plucked it out before Lillian could take possession of it.

Gigi.

She blinked. He'd written her first name on the outside. Was this card something he'd written when he'd purchased the teacup? Back when she was Gigi and he was Clyde?

If so, the words inside would have been written *before* . . . before Olivia had returned and staked her claim once again.

Gigi should burn it, but it seemed the suspense was too great, and her mother, sister, and aunt were all involved now. Not to mention their two guests, Irene and Blanche.

"I'll read this one," Gigi declared. She set the teacup back into the box, then opened the note.

The first thing she realized was that the note wasn't written weeks ago. The professor had dated it—yesterday. The note was short, as to be expected.

Dearest Gigi,

I hoped to give you this teacup under more ideal circumstances. But as you will not see me or reply to my letters, there is no use holding on to it. If you can ever forgive me, I am yours.

Clyde

Everything inside of Gigi stilled. Whatever did he mean by "I am yours"?

"Well, what does it say, dear?" Aunt Rowena asked. "You look as if someone has stepped on your grave."

"Should we get her some tea?" Blanche said to no one in particular.

Lillian did one better and joined Gigi on the settee. Their mother rose from her chair, her gaze narrowed and focused on Gigi.

"I don't know." It was true. Gigi had read the words, but she had no idea what they said.

Lillian leaned close and scanned the letter herself. Then she gasped. "Goodness. He says . . ." She glanced at Gigi.

What could she do but nod? She didn't want to read the letter aloud, so she gave Lillian permission to do so. When Lillian finished reading, everyone was silent for a few moments.

Mother spoke first. "Maybe you shouldn't have burned his previous letters."

Gigi rubbed a hand over her face. "Now what?"

"Now nothing," Aunt Rowena declared. "If his circumstances have changed, he needs to be clear about it."

Lillian gave a sad laugh. "You mean in one of those burned letters? How many were there? Three? Four? Perhaps the explanation was in one of them."

Gigi groaned and covered her face with both hands. She couldn't take this back-and-forth speculating.

"Georgina, dear," her mother said, sitting on the other side of her. "I'm sorry for your distress. We could tell the post to not let anything else through from him."

Lillian's hand rested on Gigi's back. "But first we need to get to the bottom of this. I'll go to his home myself," she said. "I'll ask him directly what the meaning of his letter is and what his intentions are."

Gigi lifted her head and looked at the women in the drawing room. Irene's owl-like eyes were wider than saucers, and Blanche was gripping the emerald necklace at her throat. Aunt Rowena's mouth was puckered as she gripped the top of her cane.

"It's too much," Gigi said. "I can't keep fighting against the tidal waves of various emotions. If he truly cared about me and wanted to court me, then a letter from Olivia would have never set him back."

Aunt Rowena slapped her knee. "You are absolutely correct. His error is completely unforgivable."

Those words hung in the air between them all, making Gigi's stomach do a slow twist.

"What if it wasn't exactly an *error*?" Lillian said in a tentative voice. "What if this has all been a misunderstanding?"

Gigi looked at her sister. "How could it be that? I told you what he said at the park. He met with her, and he said he was considering a reconciliation."

No one spoke. No one moved. Irene hiccupped but quickly silenced herself. The only sounds came from the crackling hearth.

"What were his words exactly?" Lillian asked in a soft tone.

Gigi exhaled as she tried to remember the words spoken while they sat together on the park bench. She closed her eyes, remembering that afternoon with a clarity that would probably never be lost. When she opened her eyes, everyone was waiting for her to speak.

"He told me he'd met with her and that she had changed a lot," she said in a slow tone. "He said that Olivia had apologized and she wanted a reconciliation."

Her mother grasped her hand, and Aunt Rowena nodded.

"I spoke my mind about that woman," Gigi said, pride bubbling up inside of her. It had been a moment of clarity, and she hadn't held back a thing.

"What did you say?" Lillian gently prodded.

"I told him that she had no right to ask for a reconciliation, that she was returning to him only because she was divorced and not necessarily because she still loved him." Gigi took a breath. "It might have sounded harsh, but it was the truth as far as I could see."

Her mother squeezed her hand, encouraging Gigi to continue.

"I handed the letter back, then," Gigi said. "I told him the apology might be flattering, but he shouldn't forget all she'd put him through. I could see it in his eyes that he was already on his way to forgiving her, how he trusted that she was truly sorry, that he was letting her back into his life again."

"Did he say all of that?" Lillian asked.

"No." Gigi's brow wrinkled. "He didn't say it. *I* said it, but he didn't deny any of it. When I stood to rise, all he said was 'Miss Ballard.' If that's not an indication of his decision, I don't know what is."

None of the women spoke for several moments.

Until Aunt Rowena. "He didn't deny what you told him, but he also didn't confirm it?"

"It doesn't sound like he confirmed anything," Blanche said.

"You ran off too fast," Irene added.

"Yes." Gigi's voice was very, very small.

"And because he called you *Miss Ballard*," Aunt Rowena continued, "you decided it was a dismissal?"

"Yes." Her eyes burned, and she blinked back her pending tears.

"Yet . . ." Lillian said in a slow tone, "he never actually *said* he was going back to her?"

Gigi closed her eyes, and the tears escaped. "No."

No one spoke because they didn't have to.

She opened her eyes. "What if . . . what if he turned her away?" she said in a choked voice. "And I have rejected him too?"

Aunt Rowena sighed. Lillian shook her head. Her mother closed her eyes with an exhale.

"I've been a fool," Gigi whispered. "An absolute fool." She leapt to her feet. "I must speak to him. I must go to him and find out the truth . . . to know what his note means, to understand what he was trying to tell me when I would not listen."

Lillian was on her feet too. "I will go with you if only to act as a chaperone."

Gigi wiped at the tears on her face. "Thank you."

Their mother and Aunt Rowena joined their circle. "Take my carriage, dear," Aunt Rowena said. "It will be faster than your mother's. You and Lillian can drive it. We don't have time to wait for a hired coachman."

"All right," Gigi said, heat buzzing along her skin. Was she really going to do this? Show up at the professor's home? "Wait. I don't know where he lives."

"The address is on the north side near the university," Aunt Rowena said. At Gigi's perplexed expression, Aunt Rowena continued, "Oh, all right. I'll come with you. You won't have time to ask for directions."

Gigi had stalled for two long weeks, and now, suddenly, time was of the essence.

"I will come too," her mother announced. "Someone needs to make sure Rowena doesn't exert herself."

"I'm coming as well," Blanche declared. "I must see this for myself."

"I can't be the only one left behind," Irene added. "Surely there's room for one more."

CHAPTER TWENTY-TWO

THE SUN HAD NEARLY SET by the time Gigi, her mother, her sister, her aunt, Irene, and Blanche turned onto the final street that Aunt Rowena had claimed to be the address of Professor Haskins's home. They'd already passed the university, and now the homes were modest but well kept. Lillian kept the horses traveling at a fast clip, but no one complained when a corner was taken too fast.

Gigi's heart was drumming along with the tempo of the horses' hooves. A flash of worry shot through her as she wondered if the professor was even at home. What if he was out for the evening, attending some function or other?

It was hard to tell if he was at home when the carriage slowed in front of his house; it wasn't dark enough for people to have turned on their interior lights.

"Go on," Aunt Rowena said.

"Do you want us to come with you?" her mother asked.

Lillian reached for her hand and squeezed. "You can do this," she soothed.

"What if the woman answers—Olivia?" Irene whispered. "What if *she's* here?"

"Hush," Blanche said.

Gigi focused on the door, the windows, the small bushes in front of the house. It was ordinary, yet in its ordinariness, it was also extraordinary to think that she was at Clyde's home.

She grasped Lillian's hand as she climbed out of the carriage. All eyes watched Gigi descend and head up the walkway. She paused twice, looking behind her, only to see the encouraging nods of her sister and mother, the wave from Aunt Rowena, the pursed lips of Irene, and the fluttery hands of Blanche.

Gigi took the last few steps to the door, and before she could talk herself out of this entire scenario, she knocked.

Her heart skipped at least one beat, if not more. Did she hear footsteps? Any sound inside? There was nothing. Should she knock again? Leave a note?

"Knock again," Aunt Rowena called in a not-so-quiet voice.

"Yes, don't give up now," Blanche added.

Gigi wanted to disappear into the ground because at that moment, an older couple was strolling along the walkway and had probably heard. But Gigi had come this far, so she took a breath, knocked a second time, and waited again.

Still nothing.

Perhaps it was meant to be. It was a sign. This rushed trip to his home was just that—a rushed trip. A fool's errand. She turned and walked to the carriage. The disappointment on everyone's faces mirrored her own.

"Did you hear anything inside?" Aunt Rowena asked.

"No. He must not be home." Gigi tried to keep her voice subdued because the older couple was much closer now.

All she needed was a neighbor to report to the professor that Gigi had been banging on his door. It would be best if he never knew about this errand. She could write him back—yes, that was what she'd do.

"Are you looking for the professor?" a woman said.

Turning slowly, Gigi looked at the couple. They were only a few paces away. She felt embarrassment climb up her neck.

"Yes, we are," Aunt Rowena said. "Do you know when he might be home?"

The woman's aged face lifted into a smile. "Oh, he's never inside his home this hour of the evening. Isn't that right, Phillip?"

The man beside her grunted an unintelligible reply.

"That's right," the woman continued. "He's in the backyard. Says the light is the best this time of day for his painting, you know."

"Painting?" Gigi repeated. Clyde was a painter? How . . . how had she not known?

"The professor's a painter?" Irene asked.

The man named Phillip grunted something else.

"Yes, yes, dear," the woman said to her husband in a scolding but affectionate tone. "We'll keep moving."

Gigi watched the woman and the man continue ambling along the walkway.

"Well," her mother said in a hushed voice. "There's your answer."

"Go around to the back of the house," Aunt Rowena added.

"Why didn't you tell us he was a painter?" Lillian said in a somewhat dreamy voice.

"I didn't know." Gigi glanced at Aunt Rowena. Her aunt had researched the man. Had she known?

"I didn't know either," Blanche said. "Did you know, Irene?"

"How would I know?" Irene answered in a puzzled tone.

But now wasn't the time to discuss particulars. If the woman and her husband had been correct, the professor was at home in his backyard.

She brushed her palms against her skirt, then set off toward the side of the house where she'd seen a wooden gate next to the ivy-covered wall. She lifted the latch and stepped through. Before taking another step, she turned to look at the carriage full of women. Each of them smiled or nodded with encouragement.

"All right, here we go," Gigi whispered to herself.

She followed a path of flat stones winding through rather thick foliage as if the yard hadn't been tended to in some time. The scents were heavenly though, coming from the blooming bushes and a long thicket of roses that extended beyond the house.

She slowed her step as she reached the far corner, not knowing what she might see.

At first, she didn't see anything but wild tangles of vines and bushes, but another few steps and she caught a glimpse of a gazebo. Well, it had no top, and the sides were only about waist high. Then she realized it was sort of like an outside studio.

And in the middle stood a man . . . the professor. His back was to her as he faced an easel. He wasn't painting, although he had a brush in one hand. His other hand rested on his hip as he gazed at whatever he'd painted. Maybe trying to make a decision on a color?

Perhaps she should leave him to his work. He seemed wholly focused on the canvas, and she would only be interrupting him.

Of course, once she returned to the carriage without having spoken to him, her family would probably march her into the backyard again.

So, Gigi took another step and another. Still he didn't turn, focused as he seemed to be. When she was about ten paces away, a twig crackled beneath her shoe, and he whirled toward her.

"Hello, Professor," she said, knowing her voice sounded shaky.

His hazel eyes took the whole of her in, and she gazed right back. He wore no jacket or hat. The sleeves of his off-white shirt were rolled up to the elbows, and bits of paint speckled his forearms and hands. His shirt was open at the collar, and his white-blond hair was more disheveled than she'd ever seen it, making him look like a . . . well, a painter.

How had she not known? How had she not asked?

"I knocked, but no one answered," she said. "I was about to return home, but one of your neighbors happened to be walking by and mentioned you would be in the backyard painting this time of the evening. So I hope it wasn't too presumptuous of me to come through the gate." She was rambling, completely rambling, and she wasn't sure if she'd ever spoken so fast in her life.

The professor was still staring at her.

"I received the package with the teacup." She gave a nervous laugh. "I knew right away that you must have gotten it in that charming toy shop in Vienna on the return trip. It's lovely, so I wanted to thank you, and I read the note . . ."

He took a step forward. "Miss Ballard—"

"See, I don't understand why you call me Miss Ballard now, and in the note with the teacup, you called me Gigi." She clasped her hands together because they were trembling. "I thought you called me Miss Ballard at the park because you were going to reconcile with Olivia, so I left, and . . . and then you wrote those letters, but I didn't want to read about your new life and your new decisions. So I burned all of your letters without reading them."

The professor hadn't moved after the first step, but now he set his brush down and stepped off the gazebo, which put them much closer to each other. "You burned my letters?"

She took a breath then. "I did."

His beautiful hazel eyes were unreadable. What was going through his mind? Was he annoyed? Angry?

The edges of his mouth lifted, and his eyes sparked with amusement. "You burned my letters? So you have not read any of them, save for the note with the teacup?"

Why was he repeating things? The heat that had begun in her chest was spreading outward. "Yes?"

The edges of his mouth lifted farther. Was he . . . laughing at her?

"Gigi . . ." He stepped forward and reached for her hand.

But she stepped back, moving her hands behind her and clasping them tight. "You're confusing me, Professor Haskins."

"Clyde." He was even closer now. Did he not know to keep his distance? "If you would have read my first letter, you would have found out I told Olivia that I might forgive her, but I no longer wanted to marry her. Any desire had fled long ago. I just didn't know it until I met you."

Gigi loosened her hands and set them on her hips. "You sent her away?"

His hazel eyes were lighter now, nearly dancing. "If you had read my second letter, you would have discovered that I'd invited you to a family dinner, a supper to meet my sister and her family."

"You have a sister?" Why had they never spoken of this?

He moved closer still, until she caught the scent of him. Wood and sage. And now she added paint to that scent. She still hadn't wrapped her mind around the fact that Clyde Haskins was a painter. And he had a sister. And he wasn't courting Olivia . . .

"What did the third letter say?" she asked, barely above a whisper.

He was right in front of her now, close enough to touch. Close enough to hold. "The third letter was a confession."

She blinked at this.

One of his hands strayed to hers, gently tugging it from her waist and intertwining their fingers. "A confession of how I feel about you."

The warmth of his fingers locked with hers started a slow burning heat skittering across her skin.

"Addressed to *Miss Ballard*?"

"Sometimes a letter needs to be more official," he said in a rasp, "because it's a declaration."

The slow heat was climbing to her neck. "What sort of declaration?"

"The declaration of how I've fallen in love with you, Rowena Georgina Ballard II." His lips now curved into a full smile.

"You remembered my full name," she said.

"I remember every word you've ever said." His fingers touched her jaw. "I couldn't very well marry another woman when my every thought and every desire was with you."

Gigi exhaled. Her face was completely and utterly flushed, she was sure of it. The heat had nowhere else to go. "That is quite a declaration, Professor."

"Clyde." He leaned down, his hazel eyes only inches away.

"Clyde."

His lips brushed hers then, and Gigi decided that there could be more than one perfect kiss in a lifetime. The kiss on the train, and now this . . . although Clyde kissing her now was perhaps more significant because, after all, he'd just told her he loved her.

She slid her hands up his chest, her body trembling at the solid warmth beneath his shirt, and she skimmed her fingers behind his neck, pulling him closer, savoring his scent, his taste, his solidness beneath her hands.

And then she said the words she'd held bottled up for so long. "I love you, too, Clyde." It came out as the softest whisper, but the impact was immediate.

He lifted his head and cradled her face with both his hands. He'd never been more beautiful as he was at this moment in his tangled garden, paint flecks in his hair, his gaze filled with earnest warmth. "Then you had better marry me, Miss Ballard. There is no other outcome I will accept."

"Nor I," a regal voice said behind Gigi.

She froze, every part of her going stiff.

Clyde's face went a rather bright shade of red.

Gigi spun to see that, indeed, they had an audience of five. If the horses had been able to fit through the gate, perhaps it would have been seven sets of eyes breaking into their privacy.

Her mother's cheeks were streaked with tears. "Congratulations, both of you!"

Lillian had a hand over her mouth, her eyes rounded.

Irene and Blanche were clutching each other's hands as if they needed support to stand upright.

"Is that a painting of Georgina?" Blanche asked.

Everyone turned toward the canvas in the gazebo, which Gigi could now clearly see.

It was her on the Orient Express, in the lounge car, bent over a notebook. Clyde had sold himself short—he was an excellent artist.

"It's beautiful," Lillian murmured.

"Exquisite," Aunt Rowena added.

Gigi stared up at Clyde. "You painted *me*?"

His tender, loving gaze moved over her face, then he broke out into a grin. "I can do much better now that I have the real subject in front of me."

Aunt Rowena set her hands on her hips. "Well?"

"Well, what?" Gigi choked out, not missing the fact that Clyde had not exactly released her, even though they'd been caught kissing by her entire family. His arm remained firmly about her waist.

"Are you going to give the young man an answer?" Aunt Rowena said, her mouth quirked as her eyes danced with delight and triumph.

Gigi laughed shakily. "Don't I get any privacy?"

"The time for privacy is over," Aunt Rowena said. "We've been in the carriage a full ten minutes. A minute past that and we would have had propriety concerns."

Lillian stifled a giggle.

Their mother frowned at Aunt Rowena. "Perhaps we should—"

Aunt Rowena held up a hand. "They'll get as much privacy as they want as soon as I am assured they are engaged."

The professor's arm only tightened around Gigi, and she could not imagine what he thought of all of this.

She turned to him, seeing the expectancy in his gaze. "Why did you not tell me you painted?"

Surprise flitted across his face for a second, then he smiled that smile she loved so much.

"It never came up, I suppose," he said. "Besides, it's more of a hobby. When I discovered early on that I had not enough talent to make it into a career, I decided to become a professor."

"Are there any other pertinent things about you I should know? Besides having a sister and a brood of nieces and nephews?"

"There is one thing . . ."

Her breath hitched.

"You need to know that there was never one single moment after receiving that letter from Olivia that I ever considered her over you."

That was something indeed . . . Tears threatened, and she quickly blinked them back. "I might love you even more now."

His smile turned into a grin. "That's good to hear, darling, because I think we must do this properly. I don't want your aunt to scold me any further."

"I heard that," Aunt Rowena said, though amusement laced her tone.

And right there, in the backyard of flowers and bushes, and in front of a decent-sized audience, Clyde knelt in the dirt. He grasped her hand and lifted his chin, those hazel eyes of his nearly green against the backdrop of foliage and vines.

"Darling Gigi, will you make me the happiest of men and become my wife?"

Gigi wasn't sure who squealed. It could have been her mother or Lillian or, even more surprisingly, Aunt Rowena. Irene or Blanche were also fair candidates.

But there was a man on his knees awaiting Gigi's reply. She leaned down, resting her hands on his shoulders and curling her fingers into his shirt. "Yes."

No sooner had she gotten out the word than Clyde pushed to his feet and pulled her tightly against him. His murmurings into her hair were lost because Lillian was already making plans.

"A double wedding!" she exclaimed. "We shall have a double wedding!"

ℰPILOGUE

THREE MONTHS LATER

HER HUSBAND WAS BRILLIANT, ROWENA Georgina Ballard Haskins decided. His lectures were well attended, and for nearly an hour following, students and members of the public alike waited in line to speak with him.

Gigi didn't mind. Tonight, Lillian, their mother, and Aunt Rowena had come to listen. Lillian had brought her new husband, Bart, and he'd been quite impressed as well. The newlywed couple had slipped out as soon as was proper, and that left Gigi wanting her new husband to herself as well.

But he was the guest of honor, and so she must wait.

She watched him with a half smile and a growing bubble of pride in her chest. He was dressed in a suit, his blond hair carefully styled, and every so often, his gaze would shift to hers. And she could swear he'd winked more than once.

Apparently it was still possible for married women to blush.

"Dear, we are going to head home," Aunt Rowena said. "The line is much too long tonight, and we'll see you tomorrow for supper."

Gigi turned to Aunt Rowena. It was wonderful to see her fully recovered, vibrant again, and rejoicing in the good news from a doctor appointment that afternoon—Aunt Rowena remained cancer-free.

Gigi kissed Aunt Rowena's cheek, then her mother's. Gigi took comfort in the fact that Aunt Rowena now lived with her mother, and the two were great company for each other. Aunt Rowena's more dominant personality complemented her mother's diminutiveness.

All was well in Gigi's corner of London.

As she waited, she thought back to their wedding. Yes, it had been a double wedding after all, and after Gigi had completed her sister's wedding dress, she'd made one of her own.

And yes, she'd met Clyde's sister, Susan, and her family at last. She was a woman with white-blonde hair and a contagious laugh.

Lillian and Bart had taken off for their honeymoon to Paris right away, but since Clyde had already begun his semester teaching at the university, he said theirs would have to be delayed. Gigi didn't mind. After all, she wasn't being neglected in the least.

Oh, they saw her family once a week, and once a week, they had supper with his family. And once a week, Clyde delivered a lecture. But the other four evenings of the week, her husband was all hers.

She supposed she could work on a new sketch while she waited—she always had her notebook with her. She'd officially quit her position at Mrs. Stanton's dress shop, but the woman paid her for design work. So every few days, Gigi delivered a new set of designs and was quite pleased to see them implemented.

She still hadn't broken into the men's fashion market though. Perhaps her designs would just stay between her and Clyde. Tonight, his formal jacket had a deep-green thread added to the lapel stitching as well as the buttonholes. It would take a discerning eye to notice the difference, but to Gigi, it made her proud he'd wear such embellishment.

The last of the attendees shook Clyde's hand, then left.

Gigi rose to her feet, smiling as Clyde strode to her.

"Thanks for waiting, darling," he said when he was close. He leaned down and kissed her cheek, lingering in a way that heated her neck.

"I loved your lecture," she said.

"Thank you." He smiled and offered her his arm. "I thought you might be especially interested in the artwork at the Hagia Sophia museum in Constantinople."

They strolled out of the lecture hall and into the London night that glittered with stars. "Oh, why's that?"

"You will have to wait to find out, darling," he said, pulling her a little closer.

She quite liked how he'd adopted the habit of calling her *darling*.

They walked slowly, at last together, in no hurry to be anywhere. As they strode up the path to Clyde's home, well, *their* home now, Gigi felt a rush of pride. Her husband had given her every concession to make the home theirs. She'd added new drapes and rearranged the kitchen completely.

Clyde unlocked the front door and gestured for her to step inside. She turned on the nearest lamp.

He shut the door, but before she could walk further into the house, he grasped her hand.

She turned to face him and caught his smile before he leaned down and kissed her.

His lips were cool from the night air, but that soon changed, and he pulled her into his embrace.

She looped her arms about his neck, only too happy to kiss him back.

"Why all this ardor?" she asked when he allowed them to breathe.

His brows rose. "I missed my wife."

Gigi laughed. "We haven't been separated all evening."

"When you're on the other side of the room from me, I consider that separated."

She slid her hands into his hair and drew him close again.

He kissed her, lingering for quite a bit of time, then said, "I have a surprise. I thought I'd wait until this weekend, but apparently, I cannot."

Gigi tilted her head. "Is this a good surprise?"

His eyes seemed to darken as his smile turned mischievous. "Very good."

"Well, then, out with it."

His brow wrinkled with humor. "It seems that you do have a few shared traits with your aunt Rowena."

Gigi only smirked.

Clyde chuckled and tugged her by the hand into the kitchen. There, he produced a dark-red envelope.

"A letter?" she asked.

He only motioned for her to open it, then folded his arms.

She opened the seal, then drew out the thick notecard. It was a certificate—a booked passage on the Orient Express leaving next week. "What is this?" she asked.

"It's our honeymoon."

"But this is next week—and you are still teaching."

"The week after is our fall break, and I've found a replacement for this coming week," he said, his mouth curving into a smile. "That gives us two weeks. And I aim to take you all the way to Constantinople this time."

Several things clicked in her mind then. Clyde had been planning this for some time, and tonight's lecture proved it. And he'd somehow guessed that if there was any place she could choose in the world to go on a honeymoon, it would be with him—doing what they'd done when they'd fallen in love.

The tears couldn't be held back, and she wiped at her cheeks. "Oh, Clyde, I don't know what to say."

"Yes?" he suggested.

She was in his arms in less than a heartbeat. "Yes," she said, laughing and crying at the same time. "Yes, yes, yes."

He chuckled and only pulled her closer. "I love you, darling," he murmured against her hair.

Gigi sighed with complete joy. "Please tell me that it's just us—I mean as far as our families go. There will be no added travelers to accompany us?"

"It wouldn't be a proper honeymoon if that were the case."

She was grinning now. "Not that I don't love my family or yours, mind you . . ."

"Don't say another word." He drew away enough to focus his gaze on her face. "I quite agree. We have new memories to make, my darling, with just the two of us."

ABOUT THE AUTHOR

HEATHER B. MOORE IS A *USA Today* best-selling author of more than a dozen historical novels and thrillers written under the pen name H.B. Moore. She writes women's fiction, romance, and inspirational nonfiction under Heather B. Moore. This can all be confusing, so her kids just call her Mom. Heather attended Cairo American College in Egypt and the Anglican School of Jerusalem in Israel and earned a bachelor of science degree from Brigham Young University in Utah. Visit Heather's website here: www.hbmoore.com.

Enjoy this sneak peek of Jen Geigle Johnson's Romance on the Orient Express book, coming August 2021:

Song of SALZBURG

SPRING 1900

FREYA WINTER RESTED THE BACK of her hand on her mother's forehead. "Are you well enough, Mama?" Leaving her mother while she was in a bout of coughs felt like a betrayal.

"I am well enough. We all know I will not die from this, but I envy your crisp mountain air. If I could just leave London and the filth I breathe here every day . . ."

"You could stay in Paris with Grandmother. Then I will see you when I visit from Salzburg."

She closed her eyes. "I am too tired for the journey."

"Or perhaps you will vacation to Brighton as you have so long desired." Freya hoped her father would grant this one wish. Her mother would benefit from the sea air, and Freya could leave for Salzburg with less guilt.

When her mother fell asleep, Freya joined her father at the breakfast table. He was reading the paper. As usual, he'd set the gossip columns aside, perhaps hoping Freya would take an interest in the social lives of those around them. This morning, she didn't even pick up the pages to appease him. "Mother would do well in Brighton."

"Yes." He read a moment more.

"Do you think you will be able to take her?"

After a moment, he lowered the paper, his thick eyebrows, which were perhaps intimidating to some, were drawn together. "I'm doing my best, Freya. It would help if you were also doing something."

The hurt caused her hands to clench and nearly managed to bring tears, but she swallowed twice and then sat up taller. "I will only be gone a few months."

"Yes, and what good is it doing anyone? If you would stay here, take an interest in a courtship, marry . . . I would like to pass along some of my work, then retire and go to Brighton with your mother."

"But perhaps a vacation only? And then, when I return, you might retire." This old, tired conversation seemed to be the only thing her father ever wished to discuss of late. She was not opposed to marriage, but when she compared it to creating music that carried her away, running a violin bow across strings, joining large orchestras, traveling, and playing for others, marriage just seemed . . . meant for a later time in her life. She was not entirely to blame. No men had yet seemed interested in her, not once she started talking about her music and her violin. Their eyes glazed over, and no amount of dowry could convince them that their future wife would be a musician bluestocking. She'd turned many away by her actions before her father realized what she was doing.

"It's expensive trying to marry you off. And when you wile away your time, we wait, your mother ill with the London air. And I work myself to the bone so that we can have all that we do and to keep you here in London Season after Season."

She knew some of his complaints were just talk; he had given his heart and soul to the railroad. What would her father be if not the great mogul of the Stonebridge Railroad? But she also sensed that things were not as successful as they had always been, that he was stressed much of the time and perhaps really would prefer to retire.

"And what does my violin playing have to do with your retirement?"

"My daughter, we have long given up on you marrying . . . After years of staying here, keeping a house on Grosvenor Square, building up your generous dowry . . ." He stopped talking and rubbed his eyes. "But what to do with you? You need a purpose, a situation, a living to care for you once I'm gone. And music doesn't provide that, does it?"

She didn't even feel offended by her father's dismissal. He had good intentions. Her heart was so far from railroads and gas and running companies or even in marrying that she knew she would be hopeless in most pursuits other than music.

"Perhaps if I can make a name for myself in Europe, I can play professionally. I will perform for some of the greatest names in music."

Her father waved her attempts to be helpful aside. "So you have said. And might I remind you of our stipulations? Go. Try. Play. That would be something, a life for yourself. And if you aren't chosen, if this Maestro person doesn't pick you, then be finished with this nonsense once and for all. We shall find a situation for you, a companionship, perhaps a governess position." He stared at her until she nodded. "Talk no more about it. We have agreed to let you go. You are going. Let us speak of other things."

She said no more, and he returned to his paper. As usual, nothing was understood between them, and her father showed as little interest in her music as he ever had.

She returned to her room with two hours remaining before she would go to the train station. She was all packed. Her mother was sleeping. Her father was uninterested. Her fingers ran along the case of her violin. The soft feel of the worn leather brought comfort and teased her fingers, beckoning her to open it. But instead, she laid back on her bed, the case at her side.

She knew better than to play while both her parents were home. There was no need to draw further attention to the fact that she was going to Salzburg for months. Her father's words sank deeper inside. She knew the ultimatum he'd set. She'd agreed to his terms so she could go. *Salzburg*. Then her lips trembled in a sudden panic-filled insecurity. She had no idea what she was about in the world of orchestras and European professional musicians. She barely knew any other instruments outside her own. But she had to go, didn't she? The truth of it all burned even deeper than her father's words. If she didn't go and try, she would regret it with every breath ever after.

When it was at last time to depart, her father left her at the station with these parting words: "Enjoy your time. Make something of yourself. Perhaps if this Maestro chooses you, all the time you've spent on this nonsense will serve some purpose at last. You need a place in society, a useful one."

She nodded, then turned and entered the station without looking back. She was used to his dismissive comments about her music. Sometimes they hovered above her in the air and didn't quite strike home. But sometimes, like now, they made her question every stubborn inkling that kept her playing and practicing despite discouragement. What if she fought a losing battle? What if she was as unimportant as he suggested?

She gripped her case tighter and forced one foot in front of the other.

When at last she stood on the London platform in front of her train, clutching her violin to her side, her feet would not take the steps necessary to board. Her skirts swished about her legs as people rushed by. Sometimes trouser legs forced the movement. Sometimes it was just the air that flowed between them. Her nose itched. The air felt thick, and since her train had just recently arrived, steam billowed around her ankles.

But she hesitated to board.

She had been chosen to learn at the hands of expert musicians in Salzburg, Austria, to play before kings and queens. Her violin instructor assured her he would not have picked her above all his other students were she not the best, the one who would succeed in such a venture. But she wasn't certain his knowledge of proficiency extended across Europe.

Almost all the passengers had boarded. The conductor on the platform checked his pocket watch, ready to call for the last boarding. A man rushed by her. "Pardon me." He turned and paused, taking in her face in one swift glance. His eyes lingered on her violin.

Her hand raised to clutch something at her chest, anything, even a bit of lace from her dress. The air around them seemed to catch up to his hurried pace, and she was encompassed by the comforting smells of violin wood and . . . rosin. Was he a musician?

He paused in his rushing and stepped closer, seeming to be most intently interested in her. His hat covered all but two patches of chestnut curls at his temples. The corner of his mouth lifted in a smile, and his gaze lingered. Everywhere he looked tingled with a new sense of warmth.

"Oh." Her hand moved to the side of her face.

His blue eyes danced. "Are you here to say goodbye to someone? Perhaps I might deliver a message?"

"Oh, no. I'm here . . ." She swallowed. "I'm here to board."

His eyes widened in obvious pleasure at the thought. "Well then." He indicated she should walk at his side. "We'd best be moving then."

Her breath escaped as the conductor called, "All aboard! Next stop, Paris and the Orient Express!"

The man waited another moment. "Will you be coming?" He took two steps toward the train. When it blew a loud whistle, he nodded his head once and then moved quickly toward the nearest door, glancing one more time over his shoulder at Freya.

She grabbed her skirts with one hand, picked up her feet, and raced to the train as the huge black wheels began to rock in place. Then she stepped inside just as they began to move.

"You're a brave one. Almost missed it, you did." The conductor stepped in beside her, and they both watched the platform get farther away as the train picked up speed. She stepped farther inside and stood for a moment at the top of the stairs, catching her breath. Her eyes strained in both directions for the man who had rushed past. But he was gone. Well, no matter. Perhaps she would see him again to thank him. She breathed in the new smells of the train—the grease from the wheels and the mixture of people all around her in the train cars as far as her eyes could see. Her heart filled with a surge of energy as the adventure of her life carried her along with every chug and rhythm of the train that sped on more rapidly down the tracks.

She stepped into the passenger car, holding her violin case against her chest and trying to take up as little space as possible. One car up ahead was mostly full. She looked from seat to seat. Large, plush chairs held every kind of passenger. She imagined the Orient Express train cars would be even more opulent once she boarded it in Paris. Freya smiled. This journey would be far brighter and more comfortable than she had imagined.

The faint smell of peppermint tickled her nose. A man with a pipe joined her at her side. He was cheery but dressed all in black. "You'll be wanting zeh ozher car." He pointed behind her.

She tipped her head. "Thank you." Then she turned and, for some reason, following the advice of a perfect stranger, entered the other car.

The spacious and lovely seats looked to be as those in a formal sitting room, placed together in arrangements with tables. Many passengers were reading. Some were conversing, and there were several free chairs. They seemed large enough for her violin to be placed beside her. And she did hope for a bit of tea. The closest passengers glanced up, smiled, and returned to their activities. She made her way down the wide middle aisle and found a large, overstuffed chair in the farthest back corner to sit in. She placed her violin beside her and just as she'd predicted, she and it fit nicely.

Soon a member of the staff approached, and Freya asked for some tea.

Her wide hat allowed a bit of covert staring on her part. She was mostly hidden beneath it, which she quite enjoyed. And she found the hat lovely. Her mother had instructed extra hat pins be placed here and there as a form of protection. She'd laughed at the idea at the time, especially when her mother had made her practice stabbing an imaginary person. But now that she was on the train, traveling alone for the first time in her life, she was grateful for her mother and her hat pins.

Freya adjusted her skirts and leaned back in her seat. No one here seemed to be the sort of person who would require a stab or two with the pins. And now that she was seated with nothing to do until the ferry and then switching trains in France, she began to relax by degrees. The door opened again. Her gaze flitted to the newcomer, wondering after her tea.

She sat up again immediately. The very man who'd walked by her so quickly and convinced her to follow him onto the train—unbeknownst to him, of course—was now sitting on the very opposite side of the car in a chair similar to her own. While he was as yet unaware of an audience, she took the time to peruse his well-made clothing, the jacket that fit perfectly across his shoulders and his lovely hat that hung low over his eyes, eyes that she knew to be perceptive, intelligent, and of the brightest blue.

As he placed a satchel on the floor at his feet and lifted out a book, she looked away, not wishing to be discovered in her perusal of his person. Just the very act of looking where she shouldn't filled her with an exhilarating sense of freedom. She was here, alone, traveling to another country. And even though she would have chaperones and matrons and instructors looking out for her from the moment she arrived in Salzburg, right now, these hours on the train were all hers to do with as she pleased.

The corners of her mouth lifted. Even though she might have looked a simpleton sitting there smiling by herself, she could no sooner have stopped her personal celebrations as she could the train, nor did she want to.

England moved past in a great blur of landscape. The farther away from London she traveled, the greater her hope rose within. No matter what happened in Salzburg, she was going to work hard and do her best. She lifted her chin, and her fingers itched to get out her violin and play.